SOMEWHERE ELSE

HIGHMINDS: BOOK ONE

ROXANNE WARD

GO GO PUBLISHING VW

First Publication

GO GO PUBLISHING VW

First Edition

Idaho, USA, 2023

Published March 17, 2023

Cover illustration by Ashleigh Ward

Cover design by RG Graph X Design

This novel is **appropriate for all readers**. It does NOT contain sexual encounters, offensive language, or gratuitous violence.

Genres: science fiction, post-apocalyptic fiction, mystery fiction, sports fiction, and military fiction.

file 3

TO BELLA, COLLIN, AND MAREK

In playing ball, and in life, a person occasionally gets the opportunity to do something great. When that time comes, only two things matter: being prepared to seize the moment and having the courage to take your best swing.

Hank Aaron

PROLOGUE

To cast off the loneliness of seclusion, Deegan Chance stepped out into his backyard. The heaviness of his weapon weighed on his soul as much as his body. He had already threatened the neighbors he used to smile and wave at, but survival is a ruthless business and boundaries had to be established.

He raised his face to enjoy the blue sky on the gorgeous spring morning. New buds were pushing their way to blossom in the sunlight calling the bees and butterflies to shake off the winter's freeze. He envied their devotion to fulfill a purpose without question, blissfully unaware it was all doomed. A meteorite storm was destined to strike this very day. Earth would be pelleted with hundreds of hits over the course of a week. Colorado was on the safe side of the initial assault, so the onslaught had not touched them yet. But it would come.

The irony of his self-made prison did not escape him. He labored for years to build his fortified barricade with the sole purpose of isolation while the imminent threat hung in the air, thick with slow terror. Just over a year ago, the world received the news a cloud of meteors was barreling toward Earth at 160,000 miles per hour. It tumbled the world through phases of disbelief, blaming, belief in impossible technology, depressing acceptance, and finally panic.

Deegan began secretly securing his once quaint, suburban home years before the public announcement when Dr. Seger's prediction was first leaked on an obscure science website. The astronomer had little support from his peers, but Deegan researched him, checked his equations, and found the results alarming.

First, he constructed an underground bunker, re-shingled his roof with fireproof material, and reinforced his backyard fence. He continually collected supplies to carry him and his family through the initial onslaught and the chaos that would follow. It was easy to find and secure the items on his list until the panicked realization of the public kicked in. Then, along with many others, he openly added the visible barricades. The fireproof storm shutters he had stored in the bunker went up as well as the added razor wire to surround his stronghold.

He recalled how quickly the country morphed from the normal drama of a working democracy to an oppressive regime. Information was withheld and distorted, so the public was unprepared and struggled to make proactive, logical decisions. The economy was manipulated to appease the voters' wants while destroying its ability to function. Those in charge felt they should make the life-altering changes for the once-free citizens leaving them even more vulnerable and uncooperative. But Deegan knew it was the aftermath that would send the world sprawling on its knees, and without a stable foundation and infrastructure, surviving and rebuilding were unlikely.

Looking out at his once-welcoming yard, the anguished ghosts of lazy barbeques and holiday lights tortured his memories. He missed the time when people laughed in leisure and trusted one another. He was tired. Tired of sleepless nights rethinking every provision he installed to protect his young family. Tired of standing helplessly by while madness and desperation conquered the resolve of formerly decent people.

Many of their neighbors left their homes to shelter with others combining their resources. The rest hunkered down with their meager provisions. Empty and unprotected houses were looted, and several lives were lost, but no one breached the fortified barrier of his home. It was too problematic in comparison to other targets. It pained him to think of his neighbors' chances as well as their own. But the knowledge his nation would not prevail caused him the greatest despair. Instead of a determined people working as one, humanity raged with violent desperation awaiting its fate, its judgment day.

"Honey, what are you doing out here? The first strikes are about to hit Asia. Desperates are being reported searching for last-minute shelter." Deegan's wife, Lucia called walking toward him from the backyard door.

"It's fine Lucee," he said pulling his wife next to him. "I just wanted to take in this beautiful sky and the spring growth emerging. Within the week, maybe less, the sun will become dim and hazy, and the dust will choke the life out of the new buds. Even if we don't take a hit near here, the impacts will bring dark times to us all." Her sad eyes cut through him, and he was sorry as soon as he said it. She was well informed regarding the army of destruction hurling toward the planet. It already haunted her and didn't need to be said out loud.

It was then that Rhinda, their four-year-old came wandering out in her kitten pajamas. If they survived, he knew her innocence would not, and it tortured him. He hoped she would develop Highmind traits, so she could carry the critical information the nation required to continue. It would pain him to transform her, so he could pass on the secrets he held inside him, but each member of A.L.E.C.T. (Americans for Liberty, Ethics, Citizens, and Truth) had to choose a next-generation person to groom. It wasn't just human lives; humanity itself was on the line. The project's success was bigger than the safety of one, even one so innocent.

Her sweet disposition would need to morph into a battle-ready survivor, fighting for a cause bigger than mere existence. But she had not yet shown any signs of developing the Highmind traits required. It may not show until her late teens or even early twenties, so he would wait before he found another. The cruelty of it paled in comparison to what would happen if the Corporates were allowed to take over and enslave those in its territory.

But he would not need to divulge the project or its goals until the primary lessons were complete, and that would take a couple of decades. Deegan was only twenty-eight. He had time.

"Is it over now? Have the bad rocks stopped falling? I never got to see one," the small, curly-haired child said.

"No, Rhindy, we're just enjoying the fresh air," her mother answered.

"Daddy, I wanna see the stars fall. I know it's bad, but I think it would be pretty."

"Well, tonight I'm sure we'll see some streaks on TV," Deegan replied. She had no idea how precarious their existence was. But he was determined to bring his family through. After the strikes, the real suffering would begin.

"How about today we have a picnic?" His wife looked alarmed at his careless suggestion. "It's unlikely anyone would be able to scale this fence with its defensive capabilities, but we'll stay by the door in case we hear any trouble." He looked at his wife's skeptical expression, and he tugged her a little closer.

Since the first responders were focused on protecting the hospitals and government buildings, panic caused unspeakable violence in suburban neighborhoods like theirs. Staying inside had been the norm, but today could be their last day to be outside, or maybe their last day.

Deegan had been watching the newsfeed religiously every day since the meteorite prediction was confirmed. He was glued to the fuzzy images of impending doom hurdling toward his world. There was no way to stop it, and nowhere to run. The politicians battled with meaningless promises and empty words but failed to deliver effective actions or consequences for the outrageous behaviors of self-centered individuals. Everyone wanted answers and solutions, but even the best mathematicians were powerless to fill in the details of how it would unfold. Deegan assumed they knew more than they were sharing with the public to save the safest locations for privileged families.

The scientists fought over figures and argued over results. They didn't know with any certainty how many of the thousands of stone bombs would enter the atmosphere, make it through, or where they would hit. They did agree that once it started, it would last from six to seven days, making every inch of Earth's surface a target.

Though none were considered large enough to cause an extinction event, their combined devastation would throw the whole world into the worst disaster in recorded history. The realization of needed plans came too late for many honest shoppers, and the panicking desperates often absconded the ever-dwindling supplies. Deegan sat outside on the blanket with his wife, while his young daughter chased a butterfly. He thought back on the life he was allowed and mourned the future his daughter would inherit. He thought about his own experiences and feared what the post-apocalyptic world would look like.

In high school, Deegan earned a scholarship for his baseball skills. He also tested extremely high on the intelligence quotient, and in college, he was asked to participate in an intelligence enhancement experiment. It was considered a failure when only 12% showed slight improvement, 73% showed no change, and 8% lost intellect. Deegan met his wife there, and they were among the few who noticed a cognitive improvement, but they did not reveal it. They were concerned when several other subjects in the trial developed depression, headaches, and some had seizures. Those who reported improvements were hired at top-secret firms and disappeared. As the months went by, Deegan and Lucia both noticed a significant increase, but they faked their tests to show a slight decrease in their abilities. They did not want to be registered with the Highmind agency.

Once again, he reviewed his plan. As a well-respected architect, Deegan's salary and keen mind allowed him to prepare his home and family for the disaster without drawing any attention. He thought of everything. His crawl space was excavated to build a bomb shelter and secret compartments to hide their provisions. He buried a large water tank with a sustainable water filtration system and built an extensive greenhouse complete with grow lights. He purchased dried food, medical supplies , maintenance supplies of every kind, and appliances that wouldn't need electricity. He fortified his home against looters with effective and deadly defensive technology. They had a chance, as long as the Denver area didn't take a direct hit from one of the larger meteors.

The meteoroids of concern in the approaching cloud had diameters ranging from 300 meters (approx. 1,000 feet) to 50 meters (approx. 165 feet). Most were smaller ones that would leave harmless flashes across the sky. The next sizes would either break apart and burn up or hit the ground as rocks or small boulders. Some will simply explode in the atmosphere, but the concussions from those explosions could cause substantial damage to the local area below. The combined destruction of the ones that hit could be quite significant. But the one leading the pack was over half a kilometer (approx. 2,000 feet) in diameter. Even though it was destined to hit Earth this very day somewhere in Asia, exactly where it would land depended on its composition, atmospheric variables, and angle of descent.

He blocked the disaster from his mind to enjoy their outing while Rhinda played hide-and-seek around the yard. Lucia went all out with roasted chicken, fruit salad, biscuits, and topped the event off with mint ice cream cones. They packed up when the sun began to lean heavily toward the horizon, and they returned to the artificial light of the barricaded house.

The news feed was showing the first meteorite smashing down in China's Taklimakan Desert. It was nighttime there, but the graphic illustration of the dust cloud showed how it would spread over the whole continent and head toward the Pacific Ocean with the prevailing winds. Two medium ones fell in the Indian and Pacific oceans, and moderate tsunamis were rolling toward the surrounding shores. Greece's island of Chios and Florida's Tallahassee each took a small hit, but the fire damage was impactful. China stopped transmitting communications a little over an hour later, and not long after that, most of its electrical grid went dark. That was day one.

The next two days delivered over a hundred burning space missiles pounding millions of tons of dust into the sky, starting numerous wild-fires, and leaving huge craters where life once thrived. Every day Deegan tuned into the horror of each meteorite as it smashed into the other side of the planet. And every night, he prayed they wouldn't star in the next tragedy.

And then their news went dark. No TV, no Internet, no power. The three of them had been stuck in the boarded-up house for days, and now with the dull, gloomy emergency lights and news silence, life was unnerving. Though he had a generator, the TV stations were not broadcasting a signal, so all they had was the radio. As they gathered around the table to play cards, the air raid sirens began to howl.

"Everyone in the basement," Deegan's voice was calm but firm.

They were scurrying about gathering last-minute items, but it didn't take long. They had practiced this drill numerous times. Deegan threw aside the carpet and opened the hatch at the hallway entrance. Down the ladder, they climbed to the basement room with its foreboding seven-foot ceiling. The fifteen-by-thirty-foot area was complete with two bedrooms, a kitchen, a dining set, a couch, an entertainment center, and a small but full bathroom.

The electrical grid was supplemented as needed by an innovative battery system, and the hand pump water system was fed by the large tank buried in the yard. It was a temporary place to ride out the storm, but it was not meant to be inhabited for more than a couple of months, three at the most.

As fortified as the small shelter was, the ground-shaking concussion shocked the little safe room and its occupants. Rhinda buried her face in her mother's arms with her stuffed tiger tightly tucked beside her.

"How close do you think that hit?" Lucia turned to Deegan and asked.

"Well, even though it showed the flash on the cameras, the fire alarm isn't going off, so we're okay for now. But not knowing how large it was, it's hard to tell."

Soon the muffled sound of emergency sirens could be heard outside their little world. The three of them sat huddled together on the couch for several hours waiting for the next impact to come, but the rest of the night was quiet.

In the morning, they climbed out of the safe room and peeked out the back door. Smoke was rising in a neighborhood in the distance, but the worst of the fire was subdued. A dusty haze stretched across the sky with the windblown plume heading east. Even though they weren't in its direct path, the dust would spread out and join up with the rest traveling the globe.

From now on, they needed to sleep in the basement room at night and be ready to return to it as needed during the day. It didn't matter what side of the planet they were on now. The attack was on, and rocks pulled by Earth's gravity could skip along the atmosphere like a rock on a pond to the daylight side. The next day, the power returned, and they tuned into the horror of each meteorite as it smashed into the planet. They counted their blessings every day with a prayer of thanks.

Over the next five days, the nightmare continued. The cruel skies sent hundreds more molten space bombs each pounding more tons of dust into the sky. Wildfires could not be controlled, further polluting the air. Craters left huge, black, dead zones where life once thrived. Finally, the skies were quiet. They had made it through, and they climbed out of the safe room and celebrated in the house.

The haze outside resembled a very dusty summer day, but there was no clean air on the way to clear it out, and more dust was approaching. Denver had sustained little damage beyond the small meteorite that hit the neighborhood just over a mile away. It was tragic that eight people died and eleven were injured, but that was far less than the catastrophe expected. Neighbors, thinking they had escaped the apocalypse engaged in a premature reverie.

While neighbors feasted lavishly on their precious supplies, Deegan and Lucee watched from their fold-out, attic dormer saying farewell to the best of times. The denial outside their window was nothing short of tragic. As he moved away from the window and closed the dormer, Deegan felt the holster with his pistol shift. Its power slept, waiting, knowing it wouldn't continue to sit idle for long. The festivities would end, and reality would turn on the merry band with abject brutality. Then it would serve its dreadful purpose.

CHAPTER ONE

TWENTY-SEVEN YEARS LATER

I t wasn't just one thing that went wrong. It happened bit by bit, like the block tower game, *Jenga*, that my dad loves to play. He piles up these wooden blocks in a tall tower, and we take turns carefully pulling out its bones hoping our choice isn't the one to bring it crashing down. At first, it's easy to pull out pieces without making the tower fall. It even appears sturdy through several rounds, but then it starts to wobble. Each choice becomes critical. It's not that the players don't realize their complicity in collectively chipping away at its stability, it's about not being blamed for the final attack. The tower's destiny is to fall into a tumbled pile of desolation. Like a forgotten civilization, its demise is its legacy. It always struck me as odd that absolute destruction was the goal of the game. But it reminds me of my world where we wrestle with survival, in the crumbled heap.

Denver Corporate City is our home. It is a large territory with "24,732 square miles of land and growing." I know that because the authorities brag about it on the heading of every official document and report. We are in the Denver area, but south of the city center. My granddad, my parents—Henry and Rhinda Wayther—my little sister, Meshka, and I, Connor, live in Grandad's three-bedroom house. It belongs to a sprawling suburban neighborhood with rows and rows of houses, most of which are vacant, but they all have the same look—broken down, overgrown, and dingy.

The inside isn't much better. The front room is dim with the big front window boarded up, and only a few hours of sunlight sneaks in through a small side window. Ropes are strung across it because we use that room to hang our laundry. Behind the web of ropes and hanging clothes, there are two pieces of furniture left. One is a large, limping, stuffed chair with stains and tears in the upholstery. It faces that boarded-up window like a misguided sentry. Just in front of it sits a dusty, empty oil lamp on a short, crippled table against the front wall, with broken bricks replacing two of its legs. My grandad called it a coffee table. It was meant to hold all kinds of things, even propping up feet, but is named after a hot beverage that adults drink for energy. Only the Uppers, the ones with lots of credits, get coffee now, which is strange because they don't need energy for their lazy lives.

My mom spent her childhood in this house. It was beautiful then. She showed me old pictures of how it looked. A large bed of bright, cheerful flowers grew underneath the wide front window. The lawn had lush, green grass, and the tree in the middle of the lawn was healthy and bursting with new green leaves. Another picture displayed the tree in vivid fall colors, contrasting the house, classically and freshly painted a medium gray with clean white trim, and a dark slate-blue front door.

The last picture was the oldest and the most interesting to me. The house and yard were covered in snow, and little lights lined the edge of the roof. There were three round snowballs piled atop one another with sticks, rocks, and other accessories to make it resemble a person. My mom called it a snowman and said people built them just for fun. I can't imagine why anyone would work that hard and risk frostbite to make a person out of snow. A circle of tree limbs hung on the front door, decorated with red balls and a big gold ribbon tied in a bow. My grandad and grandmother, Lucia, stood in the yard holding my mother. She was only a baby, and they cuddled her in their arms, bundled in thick warm coats, scarves, and gloves.

I was told it was Christmas, which some religions celebrated. Religion is forbidden now, so I don't know much about it. I just knew their smiles were so big and so, so...happy.

No one has the time or supplies for niceties like that anymore, my mom would say. Today, our house is battered by years of hard weather. The wind chips at the remaining paint and freckles the ground with fallen bits of color. Each speck is a cruel reminder of a different time. The siding is damaged with scrap lumber nailed in various places like scabs sealing its wounds. Weeds replace the picturesque lawn, and the fire-scorched shell of a garage displays the abuse it has suffered. But that tree endures, and every year the green summer leaves transform into beautiful reds, oranges, and golds. It gives me hope because it stands as a symbol of a better world, and it bravely waits for its return.

Grandad bought this house when he married my grandma. She died of the meteorite sickness when my mom was just a little kid, like five or six, but he doesn't talk about that much. When my mom and dad got married, Grandad didn't want to live alone.

"I have plenty of room, and this place is set up better than most." He went on, "The places you would be issued are in need of repairs you can't afford, and they are in dangerous neighborhoods."

My Grandad gave them the big bedroom, and they settled in. I share a room with my five-year-old sister, Meshka. I have to admit, she's pretty cute with her curly blonde hair and dimpled smile. She is the spitting image of my mom. Yeah, she's cute—a cute pain in the butt. She wants to do everything I do, asks a million questions, messes with the few things I own, and is constantly in my way. When she has bad dreams and cries at night, I might feel sorry for her if I wasn't so tired, but I get up anyway.

We have bunk beds, and I sleep on the top one. It's an old mattress, lumpy and sunk in the middle, but at least I have one. Lots of workers sleep on big bags stuffed with straw, old clothing, or whatever else they can find. We only have three changes of clothes for each season. Every couple of days, I do the laundry in the hand washer and dry it in the front room. I often mend the seams and patch the tears that appear after every wash. I also do most of the cooking and chop the wood into kindling for the wood stove, which is our only source of heat.

There is no place for kids to go during work times, and all adults must work. When I was born, Grandad was switched to night shift to care for us while my mom and dad worked days. Every morning he trained me in my chores as well as lessons in the forbidden subjects like history, science, and literature.

When I turned nine, I was deemed old enough to watch Meshka while everyone else was at work, and my grandad got switched back to day shift. Grandad says nine is too young for so much responsibility, but my mom says kids are older these days because we have to be, especially when they are firstborn. It was then that I gave Grandad the nickname GD. I thought it made me seem more grown up. I was confident I could handle this job. After all, I'm nine, firstborn, and though undocumented, I'm a Highmind.

I had lots of disasters that first week, and it knocked me off my high horse. That's what GD said. It meant the job was still bigger than me, and I had a lot to learn. It was a lot to take on. I was lacking in the subtleties experience brings. But the nickname stuck.

As with most Corporate territories, the wealthiest Corporate owner rules the territory, the Neighwah police the territory, and the Uppers oversee the workers. Drangers are rogue soldiers who can be hired by anyone who has credits to do jobs needing force. Uppers use Drangers as thugs to make the Dailys fear them. The Neighwah use Drangers for the same thing, but they also hire them as frontliners. Frontliners are the first group sent to fight when other territories try to take land or supplies from ours. GD calls them "cannon fodder."

Dailys are the workers. My family and I are Dailys. We must follow the rules carefully and never argue with anyone with more power, which is everyone else. Dailys are given just enough food and supplies to live on, and one day off a week to fulfill their community and personal responsibilities. Family members are not allowed to have the same days off, so we can't spend much time being together. When kids reach nine years old, they can be on their own to manage children over three years and household chores. Kids stay home until they turn thirteen, and then they report to an official job for training.

GD says I'm a Highmind. That means my intelligence quotient is well above what used to be called genius. In the last thirty years, new scales had to be created to include the Highminds. I was never officially tested, but my grandad assessed me himself. He says I need to hide my abilities, or they'll take me to the Highmind camp. No one knows what goes on behind the walls of the expansive building across from Corporate headquarters, but that's where the Highminds go when they're identified, and they are never seen again. Maybe they live better, maybe they live worse, but I don't want to lose my family, so I keep it a secret. I don't even know if my parents know; we never speak of it. GD said the best way to hide it is to speak with simple words, as few as possible, and most importantly, stay out of trouble. I'm pretty good at the not speaking part.

When Daily kids turn twelve, they have a year to find a job where there is an opening, a mentor who will train them, and a supervisor to approve it. Parents start building up favors where they work or where they think a safe job might be opening, so their kids can lock in a slot. If a kid doesn't secure work, they may get a dangerous job or be jacked into the Drangers.

Dailys are punished if they are late, absent, don't do everything as they are told, or when an Upper is in a bad mood. Some Uppers are in a bad mood a lot. If Dailys are sick, they must show up to get sent home, and when they recover, they must make up their time. Sometimes they are sent to the hospital. That usually goes badly for Dailys because they don't have anything to bribe the doctors. There aren't any old Dailys because everyone over thirteen must work, or they don't get rations. They work until they die or get sick and then die. Sometimes, I think the Uppers cause their deaths because the older workers have lots of accidents.

Every week, Dailys stand in line to get their rations, and there are no choices. They walk to their ration station, which can be a couple of miles away. Most have some kind of homemade cart or wagon, so they don't have to carry everything. Scrap wood is relatively easy to find, but it is extremely hard to find the tools and metal fasteners, like screws, nails, and bolts, to make things. We aren't allowed to own hammers or any kind of heavy metal tool because they are considered weapons, but most do. We need tools to gather fasteners from the vacant houses, but care must be taken not to get caught.

There is a burned-out neighborhood just over a mile away from us, and all Dailys are prohibited from going there. Some say it's where desperates hide because even the Neighwah don't visit it. But the prevailing rumor is that the area is cursed, and anyone who goes into it is cursed. Dailys tend to be very superstitious, and they would be happy to turn in anyone bringing evil curses to their neighborhood. I wouldn't want to tangle with soldiers or outlaws, but teasing out the theory of the curse intrigues me.

Dailys gather supplies from the ration station every week on their assigned day. We push boxes along a wheeled counter to collect the food and supplies issued for that week. Bringing two boxes lets us trade them out halfway through, so our box doesn't look too full. Even the full portions aren't enough to take away the gnawing feeling of hunger, but it's enough to stay alive and keep working. Dailys work the supply line while Neighwah soldiers stand ready to punish people who cause trouble.

Both my mom and dad have degrees from the vocational college they called the "packet college." It was all online. They never interacted with the other students. No sharing of ideas, just "read and puke" out the correct answers. My dad would say stuff like that, but not in public; he'd be punished. My dad works in road maintenance, and my mom is a data entry clerk at the Corporate building. My grandad is an architect. He went to a real college and played sports at real games. They have tested him several times trying to identify him as a Highmind, but he passes the test just enough to keep his job but not be documented.

Their jobs seem important to me, but we don't live like the Uppers. They have clean, nicely kept yards, pretty clothes, and plenty of food. My dad says if we played along with the Uppers more, we could get favors, but GD says that's a fool's game that never goes well for the Dailys. My dad knows it's true, but he wishes he could give his family more.

Uppers' kids don't work like me; they have school at the old schoolhouse. They get to play on the swings and slides and other playground equipment. Dailys aren't allowed at schools unless they work there. There is no school for the children of Dailys; we have packet school. I completed the Corporate-approved lessons on how to obey and be a good worker. The lessons do teach us reading, writing, and math, but only enough to complete the packets and prepare for a job. I try to help Meshka with her basic skills during the day, but mostly we do our approved lesson work at night.

GD and I keep my extra lessons secret from my parents. He says it would scare them to know I was holding forbidden knowledge, but GD says it must not die. It must be passed from one generation to the next so it can live in the light of day again. He told me that when he was growing up, he had the freedom to study lots of things like history, science, music, art, and even play sports. He played on a baseball team at his college, and he was good enough at it that his college was free. Those subjects are forbidden now because they "create distrust, unrest, and interfere with productivity."

My dad says it's the universal, "don't think for yourself; just shut up and work," rule. It is a dangerous thing to say. My mom says he needs to watch his mouth, or someday he'll get punished. I think we're not allowed to say those things because they're true. It is the way everything operates in our territory. We are told we're lucky because we are taught to read, write, and do math. We are told many territories only allow Dailys to have hands-on work training when they turn twelve. I don't feel very lucky though; mostly, I just feel tired, hungry, and scared.

GD taught me about history and the United States of America. It's the name of the land where we live. It is forbidden in our territory to talk of the nations and ways of the past. He said they want us to forget, so we don't rebel against their unethical treatment of us. Ethical people follow the golden rule, he said. They treat others how they want to be treated. He said there was a time when people could say and believe anything they wanted because they had freedom of speech. The citizens of the United States had a voice in how the rules of government were made because they could vote for the people who made the rules and fire them if they broke those rules.

"It wasn't a perfect system," he said. "It was messy and at times volatile. But ideas are the cornerstones of a thriving civilization. It's true some ideas and plans were crazy, and genius, and some were even disastrous. It's like everyone has their own compass for logic and civility. Though a few compasses can be compromised and manipulated by obstinance, when good people are shown honest evidence, most will make a sound decision. But ideas must be shared. All ideas, even bad ones, beget more ideas, and we can't develop and improve if we smother them."

Although lessons like that made me think, my favorite stories were about the fun people used to have. They could go to stores where they could make their own choices. There were all kinds of food from all over the world, nice stuff for houses and gardens, stylish clothes that kept people warm in the winter and cool in the summer, and toys. Every kid had some toys, and every kid was allowed to go to school where they learned all the subjects and were welcome on the playgrounds. They met friends and had time every day to just play.

There were large places where stories were told on giant screens. People had screens in their own houses too. In other places, people sat on benches and could watch actual teams play sports, people acted out stories, or listened to live music. They drove around in cars they owned and even flew on airplanes to visit places just because they *wanted* to see them. Hospitals were places where everyone could go, and the doctors helped people with medicine that worked. Citizens trained for jobs they chose themselves, and they made something called money. You could trade money for anything if you had enough. He said that some people struggled in tough circumstances, but everyone had the opportunity to learn new skills. There was something called the Internet, and all kinds of information was available twenty-four hours a day.

I remember him telling me about nations. "Huge areas of land, hundreds of times bigger than our territory, were all controlled by one government. These were called nations," he said in his influential tone. "There were three or four really powerful ones and hundreds of others. These nations traded goods and made pacts with each other for financial and sovereign protection. Where we live right now used to be the middle of a big nation called the United States. It was one of the most powerful ones, and many said it was the most powerful. It was founded on the idea that we all are born with certain rights, and we deserve to practice and share our beliefs as long as it doesn't interfere with the rights of others to do the same."

I lived on those stories and dreamed of being free like that, of having a full belly, a warm place to sleep, of playing, and of learning at a real school. It just sounds too crazy, too incredible. I'm not sure any of it is true, but it fills my head and compels me to think dangerous things.

CHAPTER TWO

G D had a room to himself, but he spent his evenings in his big, lumpy chair in front of the boarded-up front window. He called it his dream time. He'd stare right through that wood, boring a hole to a better time while I sat on the floor listening to his stories. I was always curious about what he kept in his all-to-himself room, but I wasn't allowed in there because it was his office too. I didn't have my own room, but the garage was perfect for hanging out. Most of the year it was too cold for sleeping, but it had natural light that poured in from the four side windows. It was mostly open space, but built-in containers hid the tools for our garden and other secret supplies. Meshka and I could be out there even when the weather was bad. During my parents' or Grandad's off days, they would try to give us some time to have fun and play games, but sometimes they would work those days for needed credits or make-up time.

Dailys don't earn many credits, and they use them to buy needed items like canning supplies, warm clothing, material for repairs, or medicine. Credits are what is earned beyond our weekly rations, and although some items are offered at the ration store, most of our purchases are for materials to make our own supplies, and we barter with each other. Even the Uppers trade for our goods sometimes. Though Uppers cannot force us to do labor beyond our assigned work duties, if they discover we have created a surplus of something, they can force us to sell it to them. They can also set the price so low, it's not worth making it, but it can be used to get favors too. But unless we really need something from them, we keep our crafts a secret.

Uppers are managers and supervisors, and they earn lots of extra credits. They use them to buy nice things, and sometimes they hire Drangers for security, heavy labor, or for justice. Justice is a polite word for vengeance and for generating fear to gain more power. When you don't have many credits, you need to be careful not to anger the people who have them, and that's everyone who isn't a Daily. Sometimes trouble just finds us, and there's no avoiding it.

It was almost a year ago on a warm summer evening, and we were sitting at the kitchen table playing a dice game called Yahtzee. I had just rolled three fours when we heard voices outside. Dad and Grandad got up from the table and looked out the kitchen window.

They gave each other a look, and Dad said, "Stay here!" in his I-mean-it voice.

They rushed outside, and my mom got up to peek out the open window. I saw the look on her face, and I jumped up too. Tendrils of the flames were weaving their way up the garage wall. Dad and Grandad were arguing with Drangers. My mom quietly opened the window, and we caught the conversation already in heated progress.

"This is Dannon Drive, not Danoven Drive. You have the wrong address!" my dad firmly told the fully armed Dranger in charge.

"Don't get huffy with me. We'll put this fire out when you apologize nicely," the Dranger said with his arms crossed in front of his chest. Two other Drangers stood by, smiling and doing nothing as the fire spread to the roof.

"You know I'll report this, and you'll be punished." I could tell by the way my dad was standing and almost yelling that he had reached his limit. I was a month away from being eight then and not as brave as I am now, so I just stayed inside with my mom.

"Mom, are they going to beat Dad up like they did that man in the ration line?"

Just then my grandad stepped in. "Gentlemen, it's clear this was just a simple misunderstanding. We're sorry we weren't more respectful. Isn't that right, Henry?"

"Yeah, he's right." I could barely hear my dad's words.

"Did that sound like an apology to you, JD?" the Dranger said while changing his arms from crossing his chest to resting his hands on his hips. I was anxious about the fire which was raging higher by the minute.

"My dad looked at the garage and said, "I'm sorry, I lost my temper. I apologize."

"Now, see, that wasn't so hard, was it?" and he smiled a condescending, malevolent smile. Then he signaled the other Dranger, who walked past my dad. I thought he was going toward the water truck, but he grabbed my dad's hands, and the mean one hit my dad in the face several times and then a couple in the stomach. The Dranger holding him let him fall to the ground all curled up, and then the other one kicked him in the back. "Now, don't get up until we leave! Got it?"

"Mom!" I said, grabbing onto her oversized sweater.

"Shhhh, he'll be okay if he stays down."

"Yes sir, I got it," my dad said as clearly as his injuries allowed, and he lay there holding his stomach. They got to work putting the fire out, but the garage was a complete loss. When they left, my dad sat up, and my grandad tried to calm him down. I've never seen him so angry. "They only brought that truck to keep the assigned fire from spreading to other houses. What did those Dailys do to deserve that kind of punishment? I wish I could warn them."

"No one thinks this is a fair system, Henry. It bites big time." He leaned toward my dad, and they began talking too quietly for us to hear.

Mom rushed down the hall off the kitchen, past her room and the bathroom at the end. She opened the door to the garage. I was right behind her. The whole place was black with water dripping everywhere. Blistered boards and insulation hung from the ceiling like flayed flesh from a dark skeleton, while little wafts of smoke swirled from various corners. I thought it would smell like a campfire, but tangled in the smokey wood were the putrid smells of other charred things. Grandad helped my dad to the garage. He was bent over as he walked, and when he got closer, I saw his face swelling up, and blood trickling out of cuts on his lip, eye, and crooked nose.

"Maybe I *should* file a complaint and petition for the supplies to fix it!" my dad said with anger and sarcasm. It was a dangerous thing to say out loud. He also said some other things that Dailys aren't allowed to say. I hoped no one heard him because bad words and angry threats only make more trouble.

The garage hadn't been full, but we did store some important supplies in there. Our tools for gardening, snow removal, an old tent, the homemade ball our mom made of fluff and feathers from a couple of old, stinky pillows, and other things I didn't even know about, were all gone. But the most devastating was our split firewood for the stove. It was all gone. We had some logs out back, but not enough for cooking or the coming winter season. Plus, splitting them was something we did in secret in the garage, to keep our ax and splitting maul from being taken. The blackened heads of those tools could be cleaned and sharpened, and new handles attached, but it was more work on top of our existing work. It also meant a wood-chopping excursion would be planned soon, and I hoped I could go.

The other thing that got badly damaged was my parent's bathroom on the other side of the garage wall. We still have one bathroom that works, but it was sure nice when we had two. We lost our supplies, a lot of our wood, our storage area, our tools, our bathroom, our play yard, and our few toys, and GD lost part of his home. We were told we should feel lucky that our house was saved. I never say anything, but I'm tired of being told to feel lucky. I don't feel very lucky; I just feel mad, really mad.

The next morning, I expected the stove to be cold until some of the wood out back could be split. They would wait for daytime because noises at night brought trouble. But the kitchen was warm, and a large pile of freshly split wood sat near the wood stove. GD showed me a new pile of split wood under a tarp in the backyard. The old pile of unsplit wood was still there, so I asked him where he got the wood and where he split it. He wouldn't tell me. He seems to have a lot of secrets.

If the fire wasn't bad enough, three bricks were thrown through our big front window a few days later. We knew it was those same Drangers. It was a warning that if we complained or tried to cause trouble, they would come and finish the job. It would have been foolish to complain to the Neighwah. They were the official enforcers who patrolled the territory. They were capable of even worse violence because they had the authority to do anything they saw fit, including assigning dangerous jobs that were a death sentence. Unlike the Drangers, who got paid per job, the Neighwah were fully funded by the Corporates. They possessed vast resources and fearsome weapons, and they executed "justice" with a swift, cruel hand. It was rare that they went after the Uppers, or the Drangers, even when they were usually to blame.

We had no right to complain, no right to fight back, no rights at all. The window my grandad loved to sit and look out of was boarded up leaving the room dim and dilapidated. There was a medium-sized window on the side of the room, but it looked directly into our yard's access fence and the roof of the empty house next door. He told me it wasn't the first time this window was boarded up, but I could tell he was in no mood to explain. And yet, he refused to give up. He sat there night after night, staring right through that board, dreaming of his beautiful world and sharing it with me.

CHAPTER THREE

On a sunny afternoon, my sister, GD, and I walked to an overgrown place that used to be a park with playground equipment, picnic benches, and a baseball field. He would often take us places we could walk to on his day off. This one was my favorite because we'd play catch and hit balls with a stick he kept hidden there. But I also loved the view off in the distance of the burned-out, cursed neighborhood. It fueled my imagination, and I knew one day I would investigate.

Weeds dominated the once grassy park concealing rusty bolts and pipes from a collapsed swing and monkey bar set. All of which could stab through a shoe and make us deathly ill. GD had cleared a path to the only thing left of the playground equipment. It was a tilting, cracked slide that strained to remain standing at all. We were told not to climb it or slide down it, but we could race various items to see which ones rolled down the fastest. We took mud from the puddles of recent rain, made mud balls, and rolled them in the dried dirt to help them hold their form.

I buried rocks in my mud balls and won every race until one broke open. My sister threw a fit. "You cheated!" she screamed. GD just smiled and said it was a smart move and told her to add rocks to hers.

"You know," Grandad said, "when I was young, you could find all sorts of things to roll down a slide, slingshot rocks at, or collect things in. It was called litter."

He told me of a time when every purchase came in multiple layers of disposable wrappers, and people would discard them, allowing the wind to send them sailing around. It got so bad that laws had to be made to prevent people from tossing unwanted paper and other items on the ground. I couldn't get my head around throwing away things that could be burned, salvaged, recycled, traded, or used to fill the cracks and holes in one's house. Today, there was no clutter on the streets, just the stench of filth and decay of a dying city.

I asked him, "How could people be so wasteful? How did they get so much stuff they could throw it away?"

He just shook his head and shrugged his shoulders.

Mesh was busy making new mud and rock balls, so I asked a history question. "GD, what happened to that place, the United States? What happened to all the nations?"

"Well," he started and rubbed the back of his neck, "the government officials stopped following the laws and refused to listen to the needs of the people. Everyone got angrier and angrier and started gathering into groups that hated the other groups. The same thing happened all over the world. Some nations stopped talking to other countries, while other nations made threats of imperialism and war." He said imperialism is when one country takes over part or all of another country.

"That sounds like now, only it's with the territories."

"Yes, very similar, but nations were much bigger, had much bigger armies, and did much more damage.

"How about all the ideas people could share? Why didn't that help?

"People have always disagreed, but we used to be better at listening to each other. The news and other media fed the anger between groups, and it caused even more chaos and division. People listened to their fears and not to each other. Good ideas were shut down and not heard. Some leaders made selfish decisions that weakened the country but filled their own pockets. The media began to take sides and only report their side of an issue, so many people were simply misinformed. Others sat back, not wanting to do the work it takes to keep their leaders in check. It all just started slipping away, and many people got tired of the bad news and no accountability, so they just tuned it out. Everyone knew the country and even the world was in trouble, but they felt helpless to do anything."

"They should have tried harder," I growled under my breath.

"Yes, we should have, but as bad as it was getting back then," GD said, "it was the meteorite storm that did us in. Yes, we were weakened by many bad choices, but we were still functioning. For a year, the public waited for the catastrophe, and the waiting made them more and more irrational. Then, for seven days, those space rocks pounded our planet, and it threw us over the cliff."

"We talked about planets that circle our sun last week, but they're all deadly for living things, except Earth. Are there planets anywhere like ours?" I asked.

"Well," GD started, and he scratched his head like he does when he's thinking, "some people say other worlds are spinning in space. Most of those lights in the night sky are stars made of burning gases, but revolving around some of them could be planets with creatures, trees, seas, and stuff like our world. But they are too far away to find any absolute proof. But that's science, so don't ever repeat it."

"Grandma died from meteorite sickness. What are meteorites?"

"Meteorites. They are rocks that fly around in space, but when they hit a planet, they are like bombs. There were lots of them, some big, some small, and they fell for seven days, hitting all over the earth as it rotated. They left most countries scorched and broken."

"How many people died?"

"Tens of millions died from the collisions and the fires that they caused, but it was the diseases people caught afterward that killed even more. We're not sure how many because communications between nations stopped.

Most scientists estimated it was several billion." He had a sad look, and I knew he was thinking about my grandma and his brother.

I had no idea how many a million was, let alone a billion, yet I understood it meant a lot. But what I didn't understand was how rocks caused sickness. "How can rocks make people sick?"

"Well, the super-hot rocks heated the air and ground, causing countless wildfires which filled the air with smoke. They also threw up a lot of dust when they hit, and the wind kept the air thick with it for more than a year. The smoke and dust got into people's lungs, and it made it hard for them to breathe. People were sick, but we ran out of medicine, and there weren't enough doctors or rooms in the hospitals. Then people started getting all kinds of other illnesses because even the simple issues were left untreated. Clean water became hard to find; many animals died too, and it was hard to grow crops without sunshine and water. The food ran out, and many died from dehydration and hunger, causing still more illness. All the decaying bodies caused even more illness, while increasing the terrifying swarms of wasps and other critters devouring them, and it just got out of control. Those were ugly, ugly times."

"GD, did a meteorite hit that neighborhood over there?" I pointed to the burned and abandoned group of houses that stood in the distance.

"Yes, but you must never, never go near there. Promise me you won't."

I could tell he was shutting me down, but I didn't want to be pressed into a promise. GD said I was a maybe guy. It's because I like to think through the whys and the possibilities of everything. I craved answers, so I formulated solutions and maybe lists. I couldn't see this going in the no column. It was too interesting, so I decided to get him going on what happened to the government.

He went on to explain that the governments that once controlled those huge areas, could not keep their officials employed or safe, so each state divided their land into territories and allowed the big businesses, still functioning, to help them govern different parts of the states.

"What is a state?" I was interested in the answer, but I also felt proud that I threw him a change-up before he made me promise to never go to the cursed place.

"A state, or a province as some countries called them, were pieces of a nation. They all belonged to the same nation and had the same main laws, but they were split into smaller sections that were managed by local governments."

"If they all had the same laws, why did they need to split the nation into pieces?"

"It's just too hard to take care of millions of people who live across thousands of square miles. Imagine this. If you lived for one million hours, you would be eleven thousand and fifteen years old."

It was too much to imagine a million miles in my head, but I know how long a mile is. Several times last summer, my dad and I found time to take hikes within the territory to find supplies, like edible plants, wood, and rabbits. One was almost six miles round trip, and it seemed like a long way to me.

"The government became weaker," he continued, "and the Corporates took over the territories in the states completely. The United States government was gone, and hundreds of small territories controlled by Corporates took its place. They wanted to protect their companies and their workers, so they put up barriers and hired guards to control the borders. These guards are what we call the Neighwah.

They used to be volunteers who protected their neighborhoods, but the Corporates took them over to protect the territory. Soon the Corporates started controlling everything, and workers were not allowed any freedom. When they fought back, they were executed. The Corporates closed the borders, and no one could cross. Their choices were to work Corporate jobs or starve. So, we worked, and for working we were given just enough to live on and no more."

"That's how it is now," I said. "You know, GD, this history stuff just gets more and more interesting, but it's very complicated."

"Yes, it is. Knowing where we come from helps us navigate tomorrow. Do you remember the knights' creed words I taught you last week?"

He had a persuasive, buttery tone to his voice when he talked of his other worlds. It was like he was there, walking through it and telling me what he saw there. Last week he told me a story from long-ago times when soldiers dressed in metal armor and patrolled lands on a continent far away. They had to recite all sorts of promises about being noble and fearless. Though the pledges were noble, not all knights were, but they gave their promise just the same. He said we can use the lessons of the past to fulfill these vows.

"Yes, I remember," I said, getting back to his question. "It was be brave, wise, gracious, true, and skilled." I knew the instant I said it that it was out of order, but I hoped he wouldn't notice. Not likely, though, he noticed everything.

"That's not the correct order."

"Yeah, I remember now. It was to be brave, true, wise, gracious, and skilled."

"Excellent. Knowing the order is part of the discipline. I want you to memorize these lessons, but don't ever repeat them."

I can still see him sitting in his big, old, lumpy chair with his legs stretched out onto that coffee table. His hair was dark with silvery strands mixed in. He always had scruffy whiskers because he was too lazy to sharpen his strap razor. He said the strap razors were from the old western days, and they were very dangerous. He liked it because it would last for decades, unlike the kind he grew up with. His voice was deep and sometimes gravelly when he was mad or tired. I hope I grow as tall like him. He was even taller than my dad, but not by much. I'm an average height for my age, and I'm a total mix of my mom and dad. I have my mom's freckles, green eyes, and wavy hair, but not curly like my sister. I have my dad's brunette color, square chin, and straight nose. I keep looking for my grandad in me, but maybe it's in who I am and how I think, not what I look like.

He died last night from an injury he received at his job. He was at that age when accidents happened. I don't believe the story, but they told us a person in training dropped a load of lumber, and Grandad's leg was crushed. He had lost a lot of blood, so they took him to the hospital yesterday morning. Kids aren't allowed to go to the hospital, so I never got to tell him how much I love him. I never got to say goodbye.

He died today from complications. I don't know what kind of illness complications are because the one person who would have explained it to me is gone. I never told anyone the stories he shared, and I doubt if I ever will. They are secrets that belong to us alone. I don't know if they were real or just made-up tales, but I enjoyed every one of them. And it was as close as I ever came to a history that made sense.

I finished my chores and sat on that big chair, pretending I could see out the big window at that tree. I dreamed of the world he described before greed and meteorites destroyed the planet. Where flowers grew in front of nicely tended lawns and houses, and people could talk about anything they wanted to. Kids played outside in the sunshine with toys, garages weren't set on fire for no reason, and when people smiled, they meant it. I bet that's what he did when he sat here too. I slouched in that chair, going over his lessons and our conversations in my head, so I never forget.

CHAPTER FOUR

Though the grief was crushing me, I drug myself up with the morning wake-up horn and started working on breakfast. I used the compost toilet and thought about how it would need to be emptied tomorrow and thrown into our compost box out back. I pumped the lever for the water pump, splashed water on my face, and washed my hands with Mom's handmade wildflower soap. She and several of the women who had the same day off would work together to accomplish all manner of chores. In the spring and fall, they picked wildflowers in the meadows for soaps and pest-repelling sachets for cabinets and drawers. Combining their soap-making rations, they set to the task of assembling stacks of soap bars. Most were wildflower-scented, but she also made pine and mint for my dad and Grandad. Some were grated into flakes for dishes, laundry, and other cleaning supplies. Because they had many working hands, they created more than they would have individually.

This morning, we were having the last of the bread I made five days ago. I went to the kitchen and pulled the bread and spread from the refrigerator. Though the refrigerator didn't keep our food cold, it was airtight and kept the mice, rats, and bugs out of our food. I toasted the bread on the wood stove and mixed water into the freeze-dried protein paste to put on top. It didn't taste too bad, and I tried not to think about what it was made of. It was commonly believed it was made from the rejected scraps of vegetables and animals.

Once a month, we got real meat. We wouldn't know when it was going to be issued until that day. And then there were extra Neighwah patrolling the ration routes. The Corporates knew the Drangers would rob the Dailys, which disrupted their productivity. My dad says they provide just enough protection to ensure we won't rise up against them.

The meat was frozen and came chopped or ground up. Even though it was frozen, without a way to keep it cold, we had to use it right away. In the winter we used to be able to keep it in the garage, but we don't have any place like that now. We set it in the small freezer section of the fridge to thaw overnight. The next day after lunch is done, I put it in a stew with our canned or fresh garden vegetables and slow-cook it throughout the afternoon. It was always a treat from the salty dried meat we usually got in our rations.

The wood stove needed to be constantly tended in the cooler months because it was all we had for warmth and cooking. Long ago, houses used natural gas that came through pipes that went to every home in the territory, but that was shut off just before the meteorites hit. Before the meteorite storm, GD gathered all the supplies needed to survive without electricity. He got smart things like cast-iron pans, which don't need to be washed, and they last forever. I just wiped them out with the pan rags. He thought of everything.

I doubted other households were as well set up as ours. I guess I never stopped to think of all the work GD did to repurpose his suburban home into a strong fortress and survival haven. There will never be another like him. He was irreplaceable. Our lives were bound to change in ways we can't even know now that he's gone.

For instance, I knew there were secret stash places all over the house, and I wondered if my parents knew of them all. I know we kept some dried and canned goods out in the garage, but there must be another place too. All year long, even in the winter, new supplies got stocked on the pantry shelves by the next morning. I know because I started counting. It might be in the attic, or in some hidden cabinet GD built. I knew of the ones in the garage, but there must be more. Someday, I'll stay awake to see where our extra storage is. I should know, fine, since I do most of the cooking.

Why? I often screamed inside. *Why* was he taken? But that road only led to more heartache. I had work to do, and I needed to keep focused.

"Okay, Connor, you're all set for the day. I wish we didn't have to go to work, but we both used an emergency day to be with him in the hospital. I hate leaving you today, but we have to make up our time." My mom was a worrier.

"We'll be fine Mom. Don't worry about us," I thought I sounded pretty convincing, but Mom could always see right through me. And she had her X-ray turned on when she responded.

"I know you two were very close. I'm glad you got to know him so well." She was starting to choke up as she spoke. Geez, was she trying to break me? I was determined to keep my composure; I had cried enough already.

"Stay out of Granddad's room, Connor," my dad said a little too sternly. He immediately recounted, "Your mom and I will get it packed up tonight."

I had to test this water, partly because I was not in a cooperative mood, and partly because, why *can't* I go in there? It's not like I'm going to mess up any of his projects. "If you want, I can start on it. It's a hard thing for any of us." If he agreed, it was going to kill me to go through his stuff, but at some point, I felt like I needed to do it. But if he didn't agree, I wasn't sure I was ready to hear the heated answer.

"Connor, I'm serious. Just leave it. There are papers Corporate wants back, and I don't want any trouble."

"Okay, okay."

My dad never wanted to risk trouble. He was brave enough, but not risky. Evidently, I am, because making life hard on the Corporates sounded good to me.

"Let's just not worry about it for a few days," I used an in-charge tone, and my dad was winding up. "Whatever we plan to do with…" I stopped. If I said his name, I was going to lose it. My dad saw the pained look on my face and released his frustrated mood. But my parents couldn't stay, and I didn't want to deal with the scene it would cause. They had to get to work before the shift horn rang.

"Just go, you're going to be late!"

"Okay, bye honey," my mom bent down and hugged Meshka. She turned toward me, looking at me with her X-ray mom vision. Then she gave me a hug, the kind a boa constrictor would. She held on as if I were dangling over a cliff.

Maybe I was.

Meshka looked at me with little girl eyes, hoping I wasn't as fragile as Mom thought I was. She looked scared, and I knew I had to step up, and as my…, as *he* used to say, "Just make it to first base and worry about the rest later." He taught me all about a game called baseball. He even made me a baseball. He tore up old pieces from a leather coat we used for patching shoes, and he stuffed them into a round pouch he had sewn together. He took a pair of leather gloves and sewed padding on the palm sides. He used the left-handed glove because he's right-handed. He said you throw a baseball with your dominant hand and catch the ball with a mitt on your other hand. Being left-handed, I took the right-handed glove.

"It's okay, Mesh, today is a first base day," I told her, thinking I had this. She broke down sobbing.

"Where did Grandad go? Why won't anyone tell me? I know he…he died, but I still don't get it."

She latched onto me, and I tenderly petted her head, trying to reel my emotions back. I knew if I got wrapped up in talking with her, I would lose it. Start working. That'll set me right. I needed to start the beans soaking, so I stood on the step stool and reached for the can. I was on the balls of my feet, using the tips of my fingers to roll it into my hands. I had done this many times, but it rolled to the side and off the shelf. It tumbled end over end in slow motion while teetering on the stool, I grabbed at the air to save it. I knew the noise was coming, but it was still alarming when it landed clanking and tinking across the floor.

The lid flew off and beans exploded everywhere. It was that can, that darn can. It undid my efforts to maintain control. All my pain threatened to come pouring out of me. I desperately worked to try and come back from it. Stepping off the stool, I got on the floor to begin gathering the pellets of precious food. But I collapsed, and my emotions came spilling out. Meshka knelt down where I was and hugged me, tight like a boa constrictor, like a mom, saving me from the cliff.

"He was my best friend," I confided between sobs. "I feel so lost. I miss GD so much." The pain burst forth. The dam had broken open now, and nothing could stop the words tumbling from me like beans from a can. "He was the only one who knew the real me, the only one who told me the truth about... about everything." I was sitting on the floor, gasping in small breaths, and blubbering like a baby. She put her arm around my back and her head on my shoulder. I should have been there for Meshka, but it occurred to me that she had stopped crying. She was being strong for me.

"Emotions are strange," GD used to say. "Sometimes on my darkest days, I would reach out to someone else in need and help them, and it would heal me a bit. It took my mind off myself and made me feel like I mattered. Helping others is the best medicine for sorrow."

I guess he was right because Meshka was beaming with purpose and love for someone else. Me.

Meshka and I finished cleaning up the kitchen, setting the beans in the pan of water, chopping, and loading wood in the wood stove box, making bread dough, setting it near the stove to rise, running the dirty clothes through the hand-washer, folding the bread into pans to rise again, and hanging the clothes to dry. It usually takes me into the afternoon before

I finish that much work, but after my breakdown, I took on those jobs with a fierce determination to redeem myself. Poor Meshka never made one complaint, and she tried to keep up with me. She missed Grandad too, and I need to remember that. She almost fell asleep in her carrots and potatoes at lunch. She had been crying a lot the last few nights, and she was exhausted. When she nodded off at the table, I carried her to her bed.

I had finished my jobs, and my attention turned to what was behind that door down the hall. Just ten or so feet away was the door to GD's room. I started to justify my reasons for disobeying. I wanted the baseball stuff. I wanted something to remember him by, but I knew those weren't the only things I wanted. I wanted to be in there and hold what he held. I needed to be with him and learn more about him.

I walked quietly down the hall and stood there. I was thinking that if GD were alive, he wouldn't want me to disobey my father. He shared so much with me, but not his private room. But he wasn't here, and he would never be. I needed to know that other side of him. I wanted to know the rest.

I grabbed the doorknob. Locked. *Dang it!*

CHAPTER FIVE

That first day on my own, my parents got home way after the shift horn blew. They had a lot of work, so they made up two of the ten hours they each owed. They were both exhausted, and I was hoping they wouldn't take care of his room yet. I was checking on the clothes hanging in the front room, and I saw my dad open GD's door with the key. He looked in with a sigh, walked over to my mom, and whispered something to her. She seemed to nod her head. He moved to the refrigerator, grabbed a small box, set the key inside, and put the box back on top of the fridge. He looked over at me, but I pretended to be engrossed in my work.

Score! Tomorrow I would get Mesh tired enough to take a nap, and I'd nick that key from its little box and spend some quality time with my grandad. I thought of the inquisitors, the people who solve crimes in our territory. Everyone said they just came up with the chosen lie to report rather than figuring out the truth. But I wanted to know the true Deegan Chance, and this was the break I was waiting for. I hoped my dad couldn't see the excitement churning in my head, because I felt like jumping up and down.

I had a restless sleep that night. What do I want to retrieve the most? Why wasn't I ever allowed in there? Was he hiding something, or was it really just about keeping paperwork in order? What if I find out something terrible? Even if he committed a terrible crime, I would believe he had a good reason. He was a good man, and nothing could change my belief in that. My imagination was having a grand old time ticking off crazy scenarios before I finally drifted off.

The next morning, I worked Mesh hard. We did jobs we didn't even need to do yet, but that would give me more time to explore. Mesh quickly fell asleep after lunch. I quietly got a chair and took the key directly to GD's door. I thought I would hesitate with feelings of guilt, but I opened that barrier straight away.

It wasn't too messy, but it wasn't neat either. It was dark and musty from being closed up for a week, so I spread the curtains slightly. His bed was rumpled, and the quilt my mother sewed him from all sorts of different pieces of old clothes hung unevenly along the side as if he had just gotten up.

His well-worn gray and tan jacket hung over his chair. I sat down in it and wrapped the coat sleeves around me. They smelled of smoke, pine pitch, and a hint of mint. They smelled like him. I remember how he used to boil wild mint and make a concentrated liquid. He would often dab it on his jacket to keep it smelling fresh during the cold season when he wore it too much to be washed. I closed my eyes and spun the chair, trying to dizzy myself back out of this bad ending, this death. When it stopped, I was facing his huge desk.

There were piles of papers in four shallow wooden boxes lining the back edge. In front of the boxes was his laptop. Even I was not stupid enough to touch that, but I was happy to see it was folded up. It meant no camera was tracking my movements. That was Corporate issued and tracked by them. It was probably why he preferred paper, and he was allotted a small amount each month. I eyed the papers in the shallow boxes and took the pages from one of them. The papers contained documents written in the language of his profession, but there were also drawings. I quickly figured out that the four boxes were separated by building design he was involved with. One was to repair a section of the old grain silo that took a lightning strike this spring. I remember him talking about it being finished, but maybe this was the last of the paperwork.

The next two were also repairs to buildings I recognized. The Neighwah building had plans for the unused basement to be made into three offices. Another one was for more storage room for the main ration storage center, where the rations were kept before they were sent to the distribution places. I guess my dad will take us to get our rations, or maybe he'll go by himself. So many things were going to change, and I hated every one of them.

The last one showed a new machine shop. I usually overheard him discussing his new jobs with my dad, but I don't remember him discussing this one. It was obviously his new project because there were tons of duplicate drawings and scribbled-on documents. I was sure it was one of the ones the Corporates were most interested in, so I put them back as neatly as I could.

I opened his middle desk drawer and found all kinds of pencils, and some came in colors. It also held pens, rulers, and all kinds of stuff for drawing and measuring. There were three drawers on the left side, and the top one held blank paper, graph paper, and lined paper. The second one had file folders of old jobs. I remember him saying he would look at old jobs to get ideas or reuse his designs. The bottom drawer had sentimental things, like my grandma's journal, old things that belonged to my mom as a child, and more pictures. A well-worn book titled *Sketching Techniques for Beginners* caught my eye. I knew I was going to run out of time, so I set it on the desk to check it out before I left. The coolest thing in that drawer was a green board for chalk writing. That would be nice to have too. I walked over to the built-in shelf system that went floor to ceiling and took up a third of the wall.

The shelves were decorated with several brain teaser puzzles, our baseball gear, and lots of pictures. One was of him as a young man in his baseball uniform, a frame displaying cards of baseball players, and several of my grandma. I saw a beautiful castle carved out of wood and painted with striking details, and I held it in my hand. It was sturdy and heavy, and I knew he had made it himself. GD told me many stories of knights and castles, so I knew exactly what I was looking at.

It was about five inches high and sat on a base at least six inches wide. The turrets and walls were carefully painted to look like worn stone. A little drawbridge in an upright position was flanked by drooping chains, indicating it could be lowered. A finger-sized divot was top and center of the bridge inviting the curious to unfurl the access. I carefully stuck my finger in the gap between the bridge and the wall. A sharp pain shocked me, and I suddenly jerked it back. A drop of red blood dripped down my finger. I was more surprised than wounded. But I didn't feel like going in for seconds. So much for that idea, and I wiped the blood on my jeans.

On either side of the bridge, banners were brightly painted with miniature crests honoring the royalty within. A watery mote curved from one side of the base to the other, suggesting it would encircle the whole castle had the base been larger. Poised on the other side of the mote was a dirt road waiting for the bridge to grant access. The highest tower to the left of the bridge rose high above a large bolder impaled with a tiny sword, just like in the Camelot story. Its golden hilt gleamed in the sunlight pouring in from the window. I bet that castle is protecting something in its keep, but I didn't have the time to investigate, so I placed it back on the shelf.

I picked up a picture of him and my grandma and leaned against the tall shelf. It was at some kind of gathering on a warm, sunny day. She was laughing, and he was smiling at her with an adoring expression. I suddenly was aware that GD must have been very lonely for her. It pained me to think of Grandad in that kind of grief because I know just how it feels to yearn for someone forever gone. As I turned to put the picture back, my shoe must have caught on the edge of something on the bottom shelf because I felt it catch and lift up. The basket of odds and ends sitting on it slid to the back. Then it slapped back down, startling me.

I bent down, removed the basket, and carefully lifted it up. It was a deep compartment running the length of that section of the shelf as well as half a foot below the floor. It was mostly empty, but it contained more papers just like the ones in the boxes on his desk. Among them were five different house designs. They were modest, two-story homes, but they had no kitchens. *Curious.* They were a series of rough sketches, so he must still be working on them. New construction was uncommon because why build new houses when there were plenty of empty ones that could be fixed up? Who would want a house without a kitchen? And most importantly, why was he hiding the plans for them?

In the bottom of the box, under the plans, was a cloth with stripes of red and white fabric sewn together. As I gently unfolded it, a dark blue patch on the side with rows of white stars was revealed. I held it up, and a key fell to the floor. Now, what do you go to, I wonder? Suddenly the noon horn blew. I knew I better get out of there. I thought about what I wanted from his room. He didn't like anyone in there, so I doubted my parents knew about his secret shelf. I could stash some stuff in it.

I rolled the key back up in the cloth and put everything back as it was. I grabbed most of the paper, all the colored pencils, and a bunch of regular ones, and put them in there along with the drawing book. There was still a lot of room, so I grabbed the castle too and secured the compartment. My parents knew about the baseball stuff, so I left it where it was. Quietly locking the bedroom door, I returned the key to its box on the fridge. My heart was pounding with excitement. I had just put the chair back at the table when Meshka trotted down the hall with tousled locks and bedsheet creases on her cheek.

"Want some lunch, Mesh?" I was trying to act casual, but I felt like an explorer who had just found a treasure on a wild adventure. Exciting mysteries swam through my mind, and I couldn't wait to get to them. Hopefully, I would be able to.

She yawned and nodded her head. I heated the leftover beans and rice meal for us. There wasn't much, but there never was.

Mom and Dad came home late again, but they said tomorrow they would get off at their regular time. That meant tomorrow they would clear out the room, or at least start. There was a lot of stuff in there, and it would take some time. His desk alone was a couple of boxes worth.

I was just about to ask my dad if I could help them when he threw me a curveball, as GD would say.

"So, Connor, Meshie," he always called her that baby name, "starting on Monday, that's three days from today, you guys will have company during the day."

"What does that mean?" I asked with a touch of attitude. I'm really sick of changes right now.

Mom joined the game to give me a nice, slow pitch. "It's a boy your age, Connor, named Hayden. He just turned nine, and he has a little sister who's six, and a brother, three. He needs help, so you two will watch the three younger ones together. I think you and Hayden will be great friends. It's always more fun to work with someone."

"THREE! Jeez, he'll be into everything! Can't we say no?"

"Connor," my dad said in that dad tone, "it's already been decided."

I stared at my mom pleadingly.

"Look," she said, "it won't be that bad. Their mom has Tuesdays off like me, and his dad has Saturdays off. Your dad will be here Thursdays, so it's only four days a week you guys are on your own. Please be kind to them. They are good people. Your dad works with Deke, and he's told me he is kind and trustworthy. I met him once on the work shuttle. He recently lost his wife and remarried a woman with a small child. His son just turned nine, but he's not ready to take on the task of watching both of them yet. Besides, it will be good to have an extra hand. You'll see."

"Yeah, strike one, three more mouths to make lunch for; strike two, three more people using our one bathroom, and strike three, a three-year-old to pick up after. I'm out." I expected to catch some crap for my attitude, and I did.

"Connor, I don't want to hear any more back-talk from you! It's decided. It's done. End of conversation!" My dad wasn't the slow-pitch type. I didn't want to get benched, as GD used to call it, so I decided to cooperate and change the subject.

"Okay, sorry," I took a deep breath. "I'll do my best." I watched for an opening to make my request. I hoped they would be more willing to bribe me now.

"Thank you, Connor," my mom said, looking at my dad.

"Yes, I need and appreciate your cooperation." He went back to his bowl of oatmeal, pine nuts, and dried apple bits with powdered milk. It was one of his favorite meals, and I had added a little of the honey we had gathered last month. He seems tough on the outside, but I know he has a soft underbelly, and I planned on it for this very move.

"So, Dad, I know you have to go through GD's stuff, and you don't want it messed up, but I really would like to help. And if I could, I'd like to have the baseball stuff."

He thought for a moment, and I wondered what his brain was cooking up for me. He was formulating a deal of some kind. He was famous for it. He looked up. "Well, Connor," and here comes the pitch, "I will let you help if you do exactly as I tell you. Promise you don't go through anything we don't okay, and ..." he wasn't finished with his pitch, but this was still a score in my book, and maybe he won't add the rest of the deal when he sees how happy it makes me.

"I will, I promise. Thanks, Dad!"

"AND," he emphasized, "you can have the baseball stuff if you teach Hayden how to play. You can do it on Thursdays since that's my off day, and I can watch the younger ones." He paused and looked at me, "Deal?"

I thought I was home free, but no. I was just rounding third base when I had to dash back to the safety of third. No home run this time. Baseball was my special time with GD. How could I let someone else play our game, and a rookie to boot? I know many marriages are arranged by parents these days, but arranged friendships, that's not cool. Think, think, I said in my head. And then it occurred to me, I can't play baseball alone. Maybe training this kid could work out. "Okay Dad. It's a deal." We both reached across the table and shook on it. "I have one question, though. And I'm not trying to argue, but why is it so important for me and this kid to spend extra time together?"

"I know how close you were to your grandad. I just don't want you to pull away from everyone. You should be with other kids. If after one month of playing, the two of you want to call it off, okay. But I think you'll like hanging out with someone your own age. Tomorrow is Saturday, and after work, we'll get started on the room."

It feels like everything is turning upside down. My job, my sleep, my appetite, my free time, my mood, who I hang out with, and other stuff I can't think of right now. As soon as I said it, I heard GD say, "Everything changes. No sense in whining about it. That's the game of living. Focus on what's important, and don't be a quitter. Quitters get thrown off the team, and it's hard to get back on."

Okay, GD, but can this please be the last change for a while? I need time to catch up.

No response came, just a painful silence. I miss him. I'll always miss him, but I won't be a quitter. He wasn't a quitter, and neither am I.

CHAPTER SIX

Saturday evening took forever to arrive. Although I planned to sneak back into GD's room during Mesh's naptime, I hadn't been sleeping well, and I desperately needed a nap myself. But I would get back in there tonight. I made a nice dinner of peas, dumplings, and dried meat that I slowly cooked in broth to soften it. The broth was rationed for a soup meal, but I only used a small amount, and I wanted this meal to be special. I finished every chore, and only serving dinner and clean-up were left. Nothing was going to delay this, not one more minute.

"Wow, Connor, that tasted so delicious. I think I'll relax for a bit." He looked at me, thoroughly enjoying my open-mouthed expression, and laughed. "Don't worry, we're getting to the room right now. You can join us when you and Mesh finish clean-up."

"Don't get rid of stuff before I get in there." I can't believe they were going to start without me. "Connor, it will be fine. Don't worry."

I cleaned up as fast as I could, making sure Mom wouldn't make me redo it. Mesh also tried hard to help because she was told she could see it and choose something to remember him by. We were done in no more than ten minutes.

"O... okay," I was stopped in my tracks. The laptop and all the papers on his desk were gone. His bedding was stripped from the bed, and his curtains were taken down. Mom was emptying his dresser and Dad was working on the closet. There's no way they cleared all his papers from his desk in the small amount of time we cleaned up. I went over to the desk and opened the middle drawer—empty. I checked the other drawers—empty. All that remained was a jar of pencils on top of his desk, which was not there before. He kept his pencils in his drawer.

When did they get all this done? They must have done it at night without me. Why are they being so secretive? Was there more to GD than they're telling me? They did say they needed to get Corporate some of his papers, so I guess I should have expected they would need to do that right away.

My dad looked at me closely. "What's wrong, Connor?"

"Oh nothing, I just expected it to look different. Wow, this place is so... so organized. I expected to see his desk full of work and more stuff lying around. Who knew GD was such a neat freak?" Then I looked over at the bedding, curtains, and a pair of his work clothes piled on the mattress. "I guess I'm going to have a lot of laundry this week." Dad laughed, so I think he bought it. I couldn't let him know I'd already been in there.

We spent a couple of hours packing up stuff, taking things to the attic, and sorting them into the might-need-it boxes. My mom took out several items of clothing for the grow-into and someday boxes and others for sewing material. Whenever someone died, neighbors and close friends expected a certain amount of charity, so she set aside that stuff too. She paused when she got to the pictures. I could tell she was holding back her tears, so I didn't knock her over the edge with a hug. I'd save it for later.

My mom handed my sister a stuffed bunny that had been her childhood favorite, and Mesh wrapped it in her arms, rocking it. My dad grabbed the baseball and gloves on the shelf and handed them to me with a hand-carved club. "Is that a bat?" I asked with excitement.

"Yeah, I started carving it when I saw the ball and glove Deegan made."

"Thanks, Dad. This is awesome." I was getting excited to meet this new kid. It would be great to toss a ball around. "Maybe you and I could play, Dad."

"Count on it. I've never played, but it looks fun." His attention was diverted by my mom waving him over. Whatever she needed to say or show him wasn't for me to know.

She and Dad stood by the closet with their backs turned to us and started hush-talking. It was obvious they were looking for something, and I wondered if it was the hidden papers, the castle, the key, or all of those things. I wish I knew how much GD had shared with them.

They had cleaned everything off the built-in wall shelf with great care and had turned to the closet to continue their search. It was obvious they didn't know about the secret compartment, and I couldn't tell them. It didn't take long before everything but the desk, dresser, and bed, were out of the room. It was then that my mom said she wanted to sweep and dust it out by herself. She was an emotional wreck, and we owed her some time to sort out her loss.

I took my ball, gloves, and new bat to the back porch, and I sat on the concrete steps. I tossed the ball up and down and caught it several times. I'd never play catch with my grandad again. Tears rolled slowly along the contour of my cheeks and dripped off my chin before I wiped them away on my shirt. I didn't sob or lose it like last time. This was a slow, gnawing ache and a quiet cry. I guess it was starting to settle in.

Sunday evening came, and I was trying to figure out how to prepare for a houseful of kids. Lots of families shared daycare like this. It allowed one person to do a chore or go some place without dragging little ones along. Maybe it will be easier with Hayden. Mesh was a pretty easy kid, even though she wanted to do everything and go everywhere I did.

I was gathering tomorrow's laundry after my dad came home and changed out of his work clothes. His clothes got really dirty working on the road crew, but Mom's job was working inside on a computer, so hers didn't need to be washed as often. My parents looked particularly excited about something when they called me into the kitchen.

"So," my dad began, "since you have been so helpful and cooperative about the chores around here. And because you're going to have more responsibilities tomorrow, we have a surprise for you. Follow me."

What in the world was up? Dad seemed almost giddy. "Connor," Mom said as I followed them down to stand in front of GD's room, "this is your new room, your own room."

I was floored. "Really! No kidding! Oh, my gosh!" I dropped the clothes I forgot I still had in my hands right in the middle of the doorway and stepped over the heap. I couldn't believe it. "Thanks! Man, my own room!" I was overwhelmed, having my own room, GD's room. It was the best thing that had happened to me in a long time. I couldn't wait to start my investigation to find the keyhole and revisit the beautiful castle.

After dinner, I went in and lay on his bed, no, my bed. It was more comfortable than mine. The desk was empty except for the medium-sized chalkboard. White chunks of soft chalk and an assortment of detail pens lay next to it, and I drew a line on the board and erased it with the rag sitting on the edge of the desk. I remember finding his chalkboard, and now it was mine. I imagined all the things I could draw and write on it. This is mind-blowing! It was like the Jenga tower had rebuilt itself a little that day.

I moved my few belongings into my new room and began settling in. I was dying to check out the secret shelf, but I had to wait until bedtime. Then I could close the door and say I was changing. Mesh came in, and I could tell she was not as happy as I was.

"I will try not to be scared at night, but I might be." She looked at me with those big blue eyes as one of her ringlets escaped her ear and tumbled across her forehead.

"I'll leave my door open at night, so you can visit me if you're scared. Okay?"

"Okay," she smiled, returning the dimples to her face.

"But if my door is closed, you have to knock. Deal?"

"Deal," and she put out her hand, mimicking Dad and me, so I did the same.

In my room, I lit the safe candle. It was a rounded ceramic bowl that was flat and weighted on the bottom, making it hard to tip over. The sides were high to keep the flame from getting near anything, and if it did roll, the melted wax would put out the flame. A friend of my dad's worked in the pottery shack, and he made them for us after our garage burned down. Even though that wasn't the cause, it was a kind gesture, and we in turn helped his family.

As mean as the territory could be for Dailys, we stick together and try to help each other when we can. But if someone is doing something that could get them in trouble, everyone stays away and leaves them to the cruelty of the times. I don't mean the kind of wrongdoings like making a couple of candleholders with leftover clay or nicking salvage wood from the Corporate scrap pile. I mean real trouble, like secret keys and hidden paperwork.

That night, I quietly walked over to the shelf, making sure to avoid the creaky floorboards. I approached the third cubby on the bottom of the shelf and lifted the board. Everything was still there. I unwrapped the key, getting a good look at it for the first time. It looked old-fashioned, like no key I had ever seen. The metal was a tarnished bronze color. A thin grey ribbon looped through the ring-shaped top. The long part of the key ended with three rectangular bars of various sizes protruding off the side near the end.

I should probably tell my parents. I think it was what they were looking for. If I can't figure out what it goes to, I'll let them know I found it. But I want a few days to look around myself. I love a mystery, and I'm determined to figure out what that key goes to. Maybe it will explain the strange houses with no kitchens.

CHAPTER SEVEN

Monday morning started early for me, which was fine because I couldn't sleep, anyway. Besides having my whole workload doubled and strangers in our home, that little key kept knocking on my curiosity. I was hoping tomorrow I could work that problem out by getting Mom and Mesh to go somewhere for a while. She was talking to Dad about ration day, but I missed too much of the conversation to get any answers. Besides, ration day was Thursday, so it wouldn't help.

I wondered what this Hayden kid would be like. I thought back to how I was before I turned nine. My grandad was home training me, and I had a lot more time to be a kid. I helped with chores enough to learn the steps and the routine of the day, but then I had time to myself while he finished up. He taught me how to keep Mesh busy helping or entertained where I could see what she was doing. By the time I turned nine, I was well-versed in the expectations of managing a household. When my first week on my own came, I felt very confident, more like overconfident.

The first week or so was brutal. I thought I could get stuff done quicker by skipping certain steps. I thought I could save time by only putting the clothes through the wringer once, and they dripped all over the front room and didn't dry until the next morning. I burnt the bread and set a kitchen towel on fire. I left a mess in the kitchen after lunch, telling myself I'd clean it up after Mesh and I took a nap. I needed naps then. I got up and caught a rat scurrying out to the burnt garage through the door that I must have left open. I remember thinking that the job was too much for me. It scared me because we had no other choice. I had to grow up and step up.

But this kid's whole world had twisted him in knots. He lost his mom and was sent to a neighbor's house while his dad worked. Then he gained a new mom and a toddler brother. I'm sure he must have been scared of spending his first week alone. But now, he was being sent to a stranger's house, and I'm sure he wondered how I'd treat him and his siblings. I started feeling bad for him instead of threatened. GD's voice was ringing in my head. "Time to step up, kid. Knock this thing out of the park."

I had already made my bread dough, set it to rise, made and cleaned up breakfast, and gathered wood from our woodshed in the backyard. I wasn't sure how the food sharing was going to work, so I waited to see what our guests brought. Mom was braiding Meshka's hair, and Dad was chopping more wood. It was late spring, but it still got pretty cold before the midday sun kicked in, so I had a nice fire stoked in the wood stove when the expected knock came at the door.

Five huddled faces stood on the porch. I led them through the front room and back to the large kitchen and dining area. "Come in, come in, the wood stove is nice and warm," I said.

The father was medium height with a bronzed, weathered face from a combination of his heritage and long hours of working outside. He handed me a couple of totes that I assumed were food and clothing. He was close to my parents' age, but the woman looked much younger. The boy, my age, and the girl looked like their dad, with thick brown wavy hair, bronzed skin tone, brown eyes, and a medium build. The youngest boy had jet-black hair and big almond-shaped eyes like his mom. I knew that they had blended their families together, but I didn't know the details of the unfortunate events.

Dailys didn't have more than two kids because they could only get rations for two. And all adults had to go to work, or no rations were issued at all. But in blended families, parents are allowed rations for up to three children. Dailys weren't allowed to divorce like the Uppers. So, a parent was usually single because a spouse died or was one of the missing ones. It was the term for Dailys that we secretly hoped had escaped, but the prevalent rumor was they had been murdered and disposed of.

My dad told me widows and widowers who had little children were only given three months to grieve and find a new spouse unless they had someone to watch them. A report released the names of those recently widowed and ways to contact them. If they couldn't find a way to return to work within three months, their children would be put up for adoption if they did not arrange daycare. Even if daycare could be found, it was difficult to survive as a single parent of young children, so most widows and widowers with kids quickly remarried.

"Hi, I'm Connor," I said just as the rest of my crew had come into the kitchen.

"Hi, I'm Deke," said the father. "This is my wife, Maylee, my son Hayden, my daughter Savannah, and this little guy is Dace." I could see Savannah was not shy. She walked over to Mesh right away. Maylee stood silently beside her new husband. She was too thin, even for current times. Her delicate features and frail frame made me want to help her. I hoped this Deke guy treated her well, but when a loud noise outside startled her, she leaped to cling to her husband. He held her close and smiled.

"I'll take good care of them today," I said, hoping it would improve her mood.

"Thank you, Connor. I believe you will," she answered, and she smiled a small, gracious smile. A silent understanding of what they were risking and what I was entrusted to do hung in the air.

"I like your hair," Savannah said rather loudly to break the heavy mood. She was looking at Mesh and twirling the curls that hung outside her braid. My sister smiled at the bold, dark-haired little girl with a wide-cheeked smile and kind brown eyes. It gave me hope that they would occupy each other instead of tagging along after us while we worked. Now I just hoped Hayden was a good worker, and Dace wasn't too much trouble.

We hugged our parents as they said their goodbyes. Dace started to cry quietly as he hid behind Hayden and watched his mother walk out the door. Savannah was watching Meshka, while Hayden and I had our own stare-down going. He was not quite as tall as me, but not much shorter. His eyes were a deep brown, and his skin looked like bread when it was baked to a perfectly golden color. He had wavy brunette hair, wavier than mine, but not as curly as Meshka's.

"So," I decided to break the silence, "why don't we see what you brought in those totes, so we can settle you in and plan our day." I looked in one tote, and it contained food for lunch. The other one was quite full and had various items of clothing. Great, I already had a big laundry task ahead of me. Sooo many things I would rather do than more work. We'd be lucky to play ball on Thursday. That little key started knocking again, and I wondered how I would ever get to it.

"This must be your laundry—did you bring soap?" I asked him.

"Maylee said it's in the bottom," Hayden answered.

"Oh, okay, we'll look for it later when we start the wash. So, I hear you just recently turned nine. I assume you can clean, but can you cook or chop kindling?"

"I am getting better at chopping kindling, and I can cook some stuff."

"Okay, let's see what you brought for lunch. Oh, hey we have oatmeal too. Let's just cook it all together. That will be a lot easier. In fact, we should plan our lunches that way all the time. What do you say?"

"Yeah, that will work," Hayden thought about it for a quick second and added, "if we have the same stuff."

"Good point," I added. He seems smart. When we go through the ration line, everyone gets the same items, but it might be different on different days. "We get ours on Thursday since my grandad died." Saying his name still sent a stab of sadness and even anger through me.

"We get ours on Tuesday. My mom goes with our neighbor while I stay home with the kids."

"My mom has Tuesdays off too, but my dad goes on his days every Thursday. It would be nice if we could change, but it was a pain to switch days when we had a good reason, and they cheated us out of a day's rations. We'll try to have the same stuff, or we'll figure it out as it comes." I was sorting the laundry when I noticed Dace still clinging to Hayden. "Hey, Dace, I'm Connor. Do you want to help me?" He started pouting his lip, and I knew that crying noise was on its way. "Okay, look Dace I know this is a big change for you, but crying won't help. GD used to say everything changes. No sense in whining about it."

Hayden grinned a little and bent down to take off the toddler's jacket. "It's okay, Dace, we came here to play some games. Wana play a game?"

Dace nodded his head and said, "Wolly."

"Oh, sorry, Bud," Hayden answered, "I left the rolly can at home."

"I think I have something." They both followed me to the cupboard. "It hasn't been used for years," I said and held out a short tin cup. "I think it was for tea, but where the handle came off, it leaks. It's perfect for rolling, though."

Dace smiled and reached up to take the cup, needing both hands to hold on to it. He wandered off toward the sound of his sister's voice. "How long ago did he die, your grandfather?" Hayden asked.

"A little over a week ago," I answered while beginning to make laundry piles on the kitchen floor.

"Oh, yeah, that's still new then. Sorry. I lost my mom this winter. She fought a bad cold at home for a week. We finally took her to the hospital, but she didn't make it." Hayden began taking clothing out of his tote to divide it into piles.

"That seems to happen a lot. Daily's go in, but they don't come out. My grandfather was hurt at a construction site when a load of lumber fell on him. He went to the hospital too and never came home."

"It's been four months, and in some ways, it seems like forever ago because everything has changed, but it still makes me sad like it happened yesterday." Hayden tossed some more clothes in the pile. "Dace's dad died from a lumber accident too, but it was in the woods. He never made it to a hospital. He died a couple of months after my mom did. They met through the marriage list. She watched us during the day and went to work when he got home. She would get home and sleep, and my dad would wake her up before he left for work. When I turned nine, she had to change to day shift like my dad."

"Yeah, that's the schedule we had too. Did you know her before?"

"No, he just came home with her one day, but she's really nice, so I guess I'm lucky. That's what my dad says, anyway."

"Yeah, funny how they throw that word, lucky, around."

I looked over and saw Dace crawling around, rolling the cup as he went. The girls seemed to be getting along too.

"Hey, while these guys are busy, let's start the laundry. We can combine this last load, so we don't waste time or soap. I have quite a bit because we just cleaned out my grandad's room, but I won't do it all today."

I wheeled the clothes wringer out of the closet along with two large basins. Hayden was already dumping the heated water I had put on the stove into the first basin. Then he worked the pump to refill them. I stirred in some cold water so it wouldn't burn us and began churning the clothes and scrubbing them on the washboard. Hayden filled the second basin the same way, without soap.

"Why don't you check on the kids while I begin wringing out the water." I took the first item and began to crank it through the two rollers that squeezed the water back into the soapy basin and fed the wrung clothing into the clean rinse water basin. It made me ponder the electric machines GD talked about.

"All I had to do," GD boasted, "was put in the dirty clothes, some detergent, and push a button. When it was done, I'd throw them in the dryer and push another button. Folding and putting them away was the only work to laundry back then."

Hayden came back and began dunking the clothes in and out of the clean rinse water to rinse the soap out. When he was done, I fed them back through the same side, mixing the rinse water, now full of soap, with my original soapy water. Hayden grabbed them on the other side and put them in a basket. When he had the first load done, I showed him our front room drying area, and he started hanging them up with clothespins. It was getting warm by then, so I opened the side window in the front room and all the kitchen windows to help dry them faster. Then we started all over with the next load.

Watching him, I could see that he was a good worker. We knocked out a ton of work today, so maybe we'll get to play catch on Thursday. I began to look forward to it. I imagined playing catch when knock, knock, knock—that key started calling my name.

CHAPTER EIGHT

I t was Tuesday morning, and I lay in bed trying to come up with a plan that would get Mom and Mesh out for a while. I couldn't believe my luck when my mom already had an outing in mind. She was able to switch our ration assignment to her off day. Thursdays were too crowded, so they were happy to let her change. Meshka wanted to go because Savannah was going. She and my mom would be with a group, so they would be safe, well, as safe as Dailys could be. I would be home alone to investigate the key question.

"Bye, I'll see you in an hour or so." Our ration station was in an old grocery store. It was a seven-block walk for us, but some people walked much further. The stations had lots of locations around the territory. Three days a week, rations were given out at our station. Nothing was ever stored there. Big trucks came on those days, and the supplies were unloaded.

The weather could make the walk difficult, and the lines were always long, but it was getting home safely with your food that could be danger-ous. There were designated routes that were patrolled regularly, and Dailys always went in groups. Sometimes when the weather was too bad, it would be canceled. But workers could pick up one day of rations from work and bring it home on the work bus. If it was too bad for workers to get to work, they had to do without. We had built our emergency supplies back up, though the small storage cabinet wasn't nearly as large as the concealed garage pantry. But I know there is another place where we keep supplies because they keep appearing in that cabinet.

Now that they were gone, I set up my plan to investigate the key mystery. I decided to do my search GD style. It used a methodical grid investigation that started low, went to the middle, and then high. I got on my hands and knees, following a spiral pattern that covered the whole room. I was looking for a keyhole or a place one could hide. I hunted for a trapdoor under the bed, behind the dresser, around the desk, or box in a low drawer, bottom of the shelf, the floor, and baseboards, but no luck.

Okay, now for the mid-level. I searched just as thoroughly, and it took a lot more time. It seems most things are at mid-level. Then I went to the high level. That was harder because it required moving the chair everywhere I went. I was almost out of ideas when I was running my hand across the small lip at the top of the floor-to-ceiling shelf. A piece of the wood that framed the shelf was loose. My heart started beating faster. It was too high for me to see, but I carefully removed the piece and felt for a hole. There it was—a metal plate, and in the center, a keyhole.

I jumped down and got the high stepladder kept in the kitchen. Setting it up in front of the shelf, I opened the lid of the shelf and unwrapped the key from the rumpled cloth. I placed it in the hole, and it fit perfectly. I turned it one way, but it wouldn't budge. I turned it the other—*Click.* The whole shelf shifted a little. I pushed it, and it moved. I slid it over a little more, and a hidden section of the shelf from inside the wall slid out, like a pocket door. As I moved it further, it slid inside the wall on the other side. The hidden shelf was full of tubes and boxes, all taped up. It was stuffed full of them.

More plans, I thought. I pulled one out and printed in bold letters was a warning: *To be opened by trained art conservationists only! Fragile: environmentally sensitive!* What the heck is an art conservationist? GD told me people used to pay money for paintings and statues. They were nice to look at, and that made them worth a lot. The Corporate building had art, and I saw it when my dad went to register me as a nine-year-old. GD said some art was so valuable, they were displayed in buildings called museums, and people paid just to look at them.

I pulled out a couple more boxes and tubes, but they all had the same warning. I was putting them back when I noticed the tape on a square box was torn, leaving a gap. It had been opened. The box was perfectly square. I stared so hard at the tempting tear, hoping it would magically open itself. I couldn't stand it. If I had to risk hiding it, I should at least know what it is. I pulled at the reattached tape, and the flaps lifted ever so slightly. Prying the sides apart carefully, I pulled out the object wrapped in bubbled plastic. I had come this far, so I delicately unrolled the wrapping.

It was 3-D figure of a strange animal I had never seen before. It was a lizard with wings, a ridged back, and a long tail. It sat with its clawed arms curled around a fancy golden box decorated with jewels. The animal had scales the color of earthy green moss with blue streaks around its eyes and across its back. Its eyes were an intensely glossy yellow and rimmed with a dark brown ring. Its long snout was slightly open, displaying a fearsome set of sharp teeth. It was the most beautiful and dangerous animal I had ever seen.

It sat on a square base that had strange symbols carved along all sides. I looked at the precious box in its protective grasp and wondered if it opened. Gently, I tilted the hinged lid open. The sun was shining through a gap in the window curtains, and it hit the clear crystal inside, sending reflective splashes of color dancing around the room. I was mesmerized. Never had I seen anything so beautiful. The idea of people falling in love with art was much clearer to me now. I took a long look at it before I wrapped it back up as neatly as I could and slid it back inside the box.

I decided it was time to put everything back. I was replacing the first box, and I noticed a large, thin book. It said *The Denver Museum Art Collection.* I put it aside to look through and finished repacking the shelf. Satisfied that it looked just as I found it, I slid the shelf back and heard it click into place.

I suddenly saw I had forgotten the book, so I stuffed it into the secret shelf compartment. I sat on the bed and let it sink in. If that one piece of art had me entranced, what was in all the other packages? I thought about carefully peeking until I thought about how old and precious they were. What would the Corporates do to get them back, and what would happen if we got caught with it? My handprints were all over it, so I couldn't pretend I didn't know it was there. Visions of torture and slow dying gripped me, shivering through my insides.

This whole thing was turning into trouble. Finding it was trouble. Hiding it was big trouble. Stealing it was deadly trouble. What has Grandad done? I wish I had never found that shelf box. My curiosity turned to pure panic and fear. I had an overwhelming need to tell my dad. This was way over my head. But first, I needed to get the stuff I took from the shelf compartment earlier. If my dad saw it, he would know I snuck into the room and went against his rules. He would take them as protection *and* punishment. I stuffed the paper and pencils under my mattress and the castle way back under my bed.

I hardly ate my dinner, and I'm sure I was white as a ghost because my mom sent me to rest in my room while she cleaned up. Before I left the kitchen, I approached my dad.

"Hey, Dad, I need to talk with you, alone, man to man."

"Okay," my dad smiled and followed me into my room. He seemed unconcerned, thinking it was some trivial boyhood issue. I closed my door, and he saw my serious expression.

"Dad, I have something to tell you," I said and paused trying to build up my courage. Nothing about this discovery was fun anymore. The potential punishments were ringing in my head, and I started to shake.

"Whoa, Connor, what is it?" he said as he turned on his concerned parent-probing look.

"I found, I found, I think," I couldn't say it. What have you done, GD? "I don't want you to get hurt. They might even kill you and me and all of us." I felt the familiar ball forming in my chest, but I refused to start crying.

"Connor, I can see you're upset. It will be okay, but tell me right now what has happened. What's going on?"

I simply went to the shelf and waved him over. I lifted the secret shelf, removed the house plans, unwrapped the cloth, and grabbed the key. I climbed up the chair that I had left in place. I inserted the key, turned it, and slid the shelf over, revealing the hidden section. I never turned around to witness his reaction during the reveal. If he lost it, I would too, so I didn't want to see his frightened expression.

"Oh! Whoa, holy crap!" he just stared. "How did you find this? What's in those boxes? Are those tubes for his design plans?"

"I don't think so. The labels say they're some kind of art stuff. I didn't look; it says not to open it. Did Grandad steal them?" I wasn't crying, but I was trembling.

"Okay, look, I think these are the artworks that were around his business office. He was supposed to hand them over to the Corporates, but he paid for them, so he probably got stubborn about it."

"I can see him doing that," I said, but there were rows of tubes and boxes going floor to ceiling, leaving no space unfilled. His office wasn't big enough for all of that. Yet I was relieved my dad wasn't freaking out about it. That helped me stop freaking out, well, a little.

"Look, you must never talk about this to anyone, even Mom. Give me the key. Hey, what are those papers in the shelf compartment?"

"They're these weird rectangular houses without kitchens."

I could see the look on my dad's face, and it had the hint of something in his mind clicking and making a connection. The kind of look that says he knows more than he's saying or is going to say. The look that says he, we, were a part of something we shouldn't be. I suddenly felt like I didn't know my grandad or my dad as well as I thought. What does my mom know, I wonder?

"What are they for, Dad?" I asked, but I didn't expect an answer. He would protect me, and for the moment, I was okay with that. I wished I believed he could make it all disappear, but I didn't think he could. He held up the cloth and looked at it with recognition. "What is the story behind this sewn cloth? GD wouldn't hide it if it was allowed." I asked.

"Well, it's a flag of a once great nation." I could see the reverence he felt for it and what it represented. At that moment, he reminded me of Grandad.

"Was it for the United States?" My dad gave me a shocked look.

"Your grandad put you in a lot of danger teaching you things like that." Silently, he carefully uncrumpled the flag and asked Conner to hold one end. He folded it lengthwise twice and then began folding it into triangles, working his way up to where Connor held his end. He put the papers back in the compartment and the flag gently on top of them. Then, sliding the big shelf, he closed it up. I could see his satisfaction and relief when the lock clicked. He never answered my question, which was an answer in itself.

"I'll handle this," he said, gesturing with the key in his hand. "I know what to do. Trust me. None of us are going to get into trouble. But Connor, I'm serious, you must not tell anyone because then something bad *will* happen." He put the key in his pocket and replaced the wooden piece on the shelf frame. It pained me to think I would never see the lizard art again.

There were limits to his ability to protect us. I did trust he would do everything in his power, but we don't have much of that. Knowing he probably didn't know, I asked the question anyway. "Dad, what's going on? I'm not a baby. I'm involved now. I have a right to know." I was afraid of the answer, but at the same time, my fear was losing out to my curiosity.

"Maybe, some other time—not now. Tell me you understand."

"I understand," I said, looking at my shoes. But I didn't understand. He wouldn't give me what I needed to understand. All I did understand was it was bad enough that we couldn't talk about it. I felt relieved I was no longer involved by myself, but not knowing can be dangerous too. It was the only thing I wanted to talk about, but I would obey. I had to; I was pretty sure our lives depended on it.

CHAPTER NINE

All day Wednesday, I replayed visions of the beautiful lizard and the book I was anxious to pull out and read. I hoped it was filled with brightly colored, detailed pictures of inspiring art. I moved the castle, museum book, sketchbook, and drawing supplies back to the secret shelf now that my dad thought it was empty. I wanted to look at the book so badly. Maybe it had a picture and some information about the lizard.

I was also dying to investigate the castle. I was pretty sure GD had carved it himself, which meant there was probably a secret somewhere inside. He loved a good riddle, and I had come to believe this castle was a puzzle. Inside the castle's main room would be the most obvious place to hide a message or maybe a precious jewel, like the kind kings kept in their castles. It felt good to have a safe mystery to focus on just for fun. It was just a puzzle, not stolen art, crazy house plans, or a flag from a forbidden time.

It would be a couple of days before I'd be able to get to any of it though. With five of us in the house during the day, the nights too dark without lighting a candle, and the need for sleep, I knew I had to wait. On Saturday, Mesh and I would be home alone. When I get her to fall asleep, I can pour myself into both mysteries. I had never read anything about art, and GD didn't talk about it much. He obviously knew a bit about it, being an artist and an art thief. He talked about everything else, but art was skipped over. I guess I know why.

Saturday morning, I got straight to my chores. It was a bright summer day, and I took Mesh out to play hide-and-seek in the garden after we spent time watering and pulling weeds. By the time we were done with lunch, even I wanted to take a nap, but I had a date with an art museum. I grabbed the book from the secret shelf box and lay on my bed.

The book seemed unused, and the binding was stiff. If they wanted this book back, I knew I better take care of it. Although there were many interesting pictures of paintings, sculptures, and other things, I was excited about finding the lizard, so I flipped through the pages quickly. And there it was, a full-page image in glorious color. The piece was called *Vadina*. It was the name of a make-believe creature called a dragon.

"Vadina the dragon," I said quietly to myself. Even the word dragon sounded magical. On the page opposite the picture were several paragraphs and a couple of small images of the figure from different angles. Four subtitles labeled each descriptive section: *Artist, Medium, Time Period,* and *Myth.* I remember GD telling me about myths. They were stories people told long ago to explain the events in their world. I jumped to that paragraph.

Vadina was born to a war-loving tribe. At her rite of age celebration, she was granted a chest of gold holding her divinely granted jewel of power. To the horror of her kind, she was given the power of peace and hope. Being a fierce battle tribe, they worried they would be conquered by other tribes if she used her gift. Fearful that she marked the end of their civilization, she was banished from her warrior planet.

She and her magic treasure chest were frozen in an icy comet and sentenced to be hurled through space for all eternity. For thousands of years, she slept in her frozen prison. Then a cluster of rogue meteorites rushed by the comet and swept it up in their celestial current. When she was falling to Earth, the ice melted, and the heat unfroze her heart.

She found the warmth of an enormous cave created by a volcano and made her home in the wilds of the unknown land. Some say she lives there still, waiting to bestow the gift of peace and hope to a deserving generation. The treasure chest part of the myth has been lost to the ravages of time. Many different versions of its contents have been told. One tells of a feeling that sweeps across a battlefield, *leaving the soldiers unwilling to fight. Another tells of a philosophy that no one can deny as anything but truth itself. But the last describes a series of events. An absolute victory will be bestowed on those deemed the most worthy. Once the jewel of peace is accepted, fairness and justice must prevail when under its power.*

After reading about the myth, I wondered about the rest of the information. It was crafted by two artists, Fedir and Saylav Bandinski. Fedir, the main artist, was also an amateur astronomer. When he read about the meteorite warnings, he did his own research. He concluded the meteorite theory was not only credible, but his calculations also confirmed it was inevitable.

Fedir pulled his artistic inspiration from a story his mother made up for him. He sketched out several dragons and began sculpting the final version in clay. A year before the meteorites hit, he fell ill and died before he could finish it. But his wife, Saylav, also a talented artist, finished the piece. It was a popular piece and brought countless admirers to the Denver Museum.

I closed my eyes and imagined Vadina flying through the meteorite storm, clutching her precious treasure. Her tail curled and straightened as she changed direction. Enormous wings spread strong and wide, and the smoke from the destruction swirled behind her in the wind she created. She roared a fearsome sound, vibrating the air for miles as she witnessed the destruction and screams of the people. Spotting a large mountain cliff, she flew, circling the giant mountain as easily as a bird rounds a tree. Three times she flew the course, tightening her circle as she went. She heaved a stream of molten fire at the mountainside and created a vast cavern. She flew inside, and her continued demolition could be heard echoing from the hole. Then a great tumble of rocks sealed her inside, and she was gone.

I must have fallen asleep because the next thing I knew Mesh was tugging on my sleeve. I felt the book behind me, and I nonchalantly covered it with my blanket and sat up. I stretched and decided I wanted to know more about these creatures called dragons.

Today is Thursday. It is going to be the first baseball day with Hayden. I promised myself I would try to focus on baseball and not the stolen art hiding in my bedroom. It's a good thing I love baseball. I went over the training plan I had written on my chalkboard. It was the same way GD taught me. That did it. Now I'm thinking about it again. Hayden, Savannah, and Dace came to the door. Time to get my game face on.

When we had our morning chores done, my dad said we could go practice in the yard. My dad caught my attention as I headed toward the back door. He gave me a look, and I knew exactly what he meant by it—don't talk. No words were required.

I briefed Hayden on the game, but the goal of today was throwing and catching. He followed me out to our backyard, and we passed the garden. Most of the side fence was falling, and the rest was being held together with wood from discarded scraps. We squeezed through the gap in the fence that led to the yard of an empty house next door. I had cut the weeds down as best as I could on Tuesday afternoon with my nervous energy, so we could practice there.

"Okay, we're going for the basics. First, the Corporates frown on seeing Dailys having fun. They say we should be assigned more work if we have time to play. But GD and I came up with an answer. It's a stretching and strengthening exercise. Most Neighwahs and Drangers are too young to know about baseball, so it always worked. Got it?"

"Is this illegal?" He asked, wide-eyed.

"It's not illegal; it's fun. And when they hear us having fun, they hassle us. Besides, my dad already asked your dad. Just say we are building arm strength the way our dads taught us. It'll be fine. Okay, which hand do you use for eating and stuff?"

"This one," Hayden held out his right hand.

"Okay, that's your right hand. Me, I'm a lefty. So, I throw with my left hand. Stand sideways to me with your feet shoulder-width apart, and your right foot in the back. Now hold your arms out and point your front foot and body toward me."

Hayden did as I said and asked, "Don't I need the glove and the ball?"

"Not yet. Okay, point your left hand toward my glove. Now when you throw, bring your right hand forward while your left hand swings back. Like this." I showed him creating a mirror image with my left-handed style. "Now, you try."

Hayden did each move in order, taking time to check himself between steps. It was a little rough the first few times, but I could tell he was a quick learner. He practiced four or five more times, and I gave him the ball.

"Okay, now throw me the ball, right into my glove. Make sure your foot is pointed toward me." He threw it perfectly the first time, but he started overthinking it and lobbed a couple of wild ones. Within ten minutes or so, he was able to throw in my direction most of the time, but I got a lot of practice following the ball and running to catch it. It was time to show him some good catching techniques.

"Hey, I can see how this could be fun when I get better. When do I get to catch with the glove?"

"Soon. Okay, when you catch a ball, you reach and bring it in. Hold your left hand out toward me. Now keep your eye following the ball as it goes through the air, then grab it. Never stop watching it." We stood about ten feet away, and he caught it half the time.

"Now let's move further apart and try it with the glove. This time, hold both hands out, but only use your glove to catch the ball." I threw the ball, and he caught the first one.

"I caught it in the glove!" He was excited by the accomplishment.

"Great, now throw it like I showed you."

We spent the rest of our time throwing and catching. It felt like GD was watching and smiling. When it was time to come in and take over for my dad, we were laughing and beaming with confidence.

"Hayden, this was a home run kind of day," I said to him.

"I think I'm going to love Thursdays," Hayden said as he handed me the glove.

"Definitely!" Look, GD, I'm passing it on. At that moment, I could feel him smiling at me, and I wondered what he would think of me finding his stash. With the way he coached me on how to search for stuff, it's like he taught me to find it. I just have to trust my dad. He says he knows what to do. I hope so. Maybe he knows someone who can take it. Maybe he's just trying to make me not worry. But of course, I'm worried. It's a full count, two outs, a point behind, kind of inning. We need a big hit to get us out of trouble.

Later that night, I was putting away the dishes with my dad while Mom was washing Mesh's hair in the bath.

"Hey, Dad. Thanks for talking me into this baseball thing with Hayden. And thanks for introducing us. Sorry, I gave you trouble about it."

"Seeing you two have some fun being kids is thanks enough for me."

"Dad, I'm hardly a kid anymore. I'll be eleven in a little over a year."

I meant it as a joke and expected him to laugh, but he just smiled. It was a sad smile, like he was considering what I had lived through this year and the secrets I knew.

CHAPTER TEN

E ver since the secret shelf nightmare, I've tried to not stress about it. It's been days since I took out the art book or the supplies to try drawing dragons. I planned on using the moonlight since it was so bright, but every night exhaustion got the better of me. I worried about the dangerous stash on my shelf, and I knew I should let my dad handle it, but I was dying to know his solution, and was afraid dying might be the result. The "worry weeds," as GD called them, were growing out of control. GD loved metaphors. We used baseball ones to describe situations and garden ones to describe our state of mind. And sometimes we used them together.

"The weeds destroy the field and trip the players. Just like worrying will undermine a plan and zap your confidence," he'd say. "The worry weeds keep you from playing a good game, and the very thing you're anxious about happens because you focused on it. Make a plan, steady your mind, concentrate on what you're doing, and keep your eye on the goal." I'm trying, Grandad, but it feels like trouble is stalking me, and the weeds are getting taller and taller no matter how hard I try to manage them.

Tuesday finally arrived, and my mom and Mesh went to get our rations with Maylee and Savannah. My mom and Maylee were becoming good friends. I was glad Hayden had a stepmom who was so nice. Families didn't always blend that easily. Tuesday arrived, and I couldn't wait to try and draw a dragon. I opened to the section about drawing animals in the sketchbook. I found a step-by-step page on lizards. I then turned the page in the art book with the dragon art. The binding was stiff, so I stood it up and used two of GD's bookends to prop it open.

I drew a triangle for the head, a long oval for the body, long rectangles for the back legs, and shorter ones and arms. For the tail, I drew two long, wiggly lines running parallel to each other. Now the directions said to work on the details. My first attempt looked pretty awful, and I would run out of erasers if I didn't learn to draw better. It was harder than it looked, but I discovered I enjoyed drawing. I decided I would practice on my chalkboard, so I didn't use up my supplies. I didn't realize I had worked on it for so long because I heard the front door open, and I quickly put everything in the drawer.

Last week, I taught Hayden how to step into his throw to get more power, and we were just beginning to add a skip to his step. Today would be our third practice. Thursdays were something to look forward to, and I needed the distraction. I quickly finished my morning chores and climbed through the broken fence to our ball field in the vacant yard next door. I surveyed the condition of our little field and deemed it ready. I went back to have breakfast and wait for Hayden.

"Connor, there are some things I need to do in town before I can let you play ball today."

"Well, I guess we could get the laundry done." So, I got to work to make sure we were done before he came back from his visit to town.

When Hayden arrived, I was already washing clothes, and he got right to work helping. Within an hour, we had all the laundry hung up. The girls were playing with straw dolls on Mesh's rag rug, and Dace was running in and out of the hanging clothes. My dad wasn't home yet, and I was explaining to Hayden that today we were going to learn to add a skip and a step to our throw. A screech from down the hall had us leaping up and running to Meshka's room.

Both of them were crouched on the bottom bunk, staring at the dresser. "Sorry, Connor. It's just a mouse, but it ran over the top of us," Meshka exclaimed while Dace climbed up on the bed with them.

"Where did it go?" Hayden asked.

"Under there," and both girls pointed to the dresser made of scrap wood boxes on a metal shelf.

I was surprised that Dace just sat there unflustered. Instead of being frightened, he seemed fascinated by the commotion. We looked under the dresser, but there was nothing but dust balls. Mice are common but unwelcome. They spread disease, tear up clothing, make holes in the walls, and leave turds everywhere. We started looking for the telltale signs on the wall that bordered the front room. Half of it was a closet, and the other half was a built-in shelf and desk unit. Under the desk in the corner was a small, chewed hole. I lay down and could see all the way through to the front room.

"We'll seal this up, Mesh. That will take care of it," I said, knowing that mice always had more than one exit.

Just then it darted out from the shelf, prompting surprised squeals from the girls. It dashed under the bed as Hayden made a perfect base slide after it. He tried to duck his head, but I heard the thump as he smacked into the frame. He was getting up when the mouse ran from under the bed and out the bedroom door. I scrambled after it down the hall and into the front room. I slipped on the wet floor from dripping clothes and instinctively grabbed a dangling pant leg before I skidded along the rough wood floor and slammed into the wall. I saw the mouse sneak into another crack in the floorboards.

"Yeah, you better run," I scolded, "and be prepared. This is war now." I was charged up, and I thought of Vadina and her powers. "No peace," I mutter under my breath, "only absolute victory will do." I checked my scraped elbow and torn shirt as I headed down the hall.

I walked back into the room. "We took care of it, Mesh," I reassured her. Hayden's face had a red scrape and was covered with dust from sliding under the bed. He was rubbing out the lump on his head as I was evaluating my scraped-up elbow and the tear in my shirt. The girls and Dace stared at us, stunned in silence. After the initial shock, we looked at each other and cracked up laughing. A belly-grabbing laugh lasted until tears built up, and we stopped from exhaustion. It was then that my dad came through the bedroom door.

"What happened in the front room?" it was then he looked at my torn shirt and bleeding elbow and Hayden red-cheeked and covered in dust. "Or more importantly, what happened to you two?" He had that did you get in a fight look.

"We were after a mouse," I said, trying not to laugh again.

"Huh," he said. "Looks like the mouse won." He was grinning as he walked toward his room. "Better fix up that laundry before you go out to play," he yelled from the end of the hall.

"I can't believe one little mouse took both of us down," I said, and we started laughing again.

"You know that mouse isn't gone, right?" Hayden said as we left the room to get supplies for re-hanging the laundry and patching the mouse hole.

"Yeah, I just didn't want her to stay awake nights growing worry weeds."

"Worry weeds? Is that another GDism?" We both laughed as I explained the metaphor. He was getting used to my grandad's words of advice, which he called GDisms. I could tell Hayden was smart, really smart, and I wondered if he was a Highmind too.

We had just finished repairing the clothesline when I saw my dad sitting in the kitchen with his head in his hands. He looked rattled and nervous.

"Everything okay, Mr. Wayther?" asked Hayden. I just watched my dad wondering if it had anything to do with the shelf business.

"Yeah, everything is fine. I saw those same Drangers that hassled your mom a couple of days ago. They started walking my way, but they must have gotten a call. They got in their truck and left, so no harm done." He quickly composed himself, and Hayden appeared to let it go, but I knew better. I looked at my dad, and he smiled. "You boys can get to playing ball now. That is if you want to."

Hayden spoke immediately. "Are you kidding? We've been waiting all week."

"Yeah, let's go. More baseball, less talk. We're out of here." I let Hayden go ahead of me, and I turned to look at my dad. He mouthed, *it's okay* and gave me the okay sign. Either it was true, or he wasn't going to tell me. I hoped baseball would successfully distract me from growing more weeds.

We were getting better at throwing and catching. He's picking it up fast, so I decided to teach him about catching fly balls, grounders, and how to use a bat. I brought out the bat my dad made me and hit some grounders to Hayden. I decided to hit him a fly ball. He tried to move around the yard, so the sun wasn't in his eyes, but the ball went sailing over his head and out of the yard. Two Neighwah soldiers were walking by.

They turned around, but they didn't see the ball that had rolled under a bush. We crept into my yard, ran through the side of the burned-out garage, and snuck into the kitchen. We saw them look over our fence, and they pulled on the lilting fence in our ball yard. We quickly snuck into my room without being seen.

Three hard knocks reverberated through the house. My dad walked past us down the hall and opened the door. He was faced with two Neighwah soldiers. "Someone threw this rock at us!" The angered warrior said, shaking a rock at my dad. My dad turned to see Hayden and me coming out of my room.

"My boys are right here, sir. We have all been inside all day. And I would never condone that behavior." He was already rattled from his encounter this morning, but he appeared steady now.

The soldier looked past my dad and right at us with steely eyes, putting his hand on his hip close to his weapon. My dad froze, I froze, Hayden froze, and no one made a sound or a move. Time extended those few agonizing seconds until the stare-down ended. "If I find out different, you'll all be looking at severe punishment."

"Yes, sir. Thank you, sir. I'm sorry that happened, but it wasn't us." When the door shut, my dad turned in a fury.

"Dad, we have not been throwing rocks. I swear it." It was true, but not honest. Hayden shook his head in solidarity. "We came in. It's hot out there. We were in my room." Hayden nodded. We weren't lying about throwing rocks, but we knew we had barely escaped serious trouble.

"Not rocks but maybe a baseball," my dad said, and we stood there accepting the disappointed retribution we fully deserved. When he turned to go to the kitchen, we went back to my room. And the whispering began.

"That was close! My heart is still pounding."

"I was scared they were going to bash your dad around." Hayden held his chest as he spoke.

"Yeah, me too. Well, one thing's for sure, we've outgrown that yard," I said. "And we have to go find our baseball before anyone else does." I was scheming in my mind how we could get permission to go to the old ball field GD and I used. It was over a mile away, and I wondered if my dad would let us go by ourselves.

"Idiot thought it was a rock, Hayden whispered, bringing me out of my thoughts. We held our mouths to muffle our laughter. Laughing out loud would have been a great release, but we couldn't let my dad hear.

"I wish we had baseball hats," I said, trying to solve the problem of the sun in our eyes, though the sun wasn't the real issue. "They had front parts that were shaped like a hand keeping the sun out of your eyes."

"Maybe we should try to make some," Hayden added.

"Yeah, but first, we need to get that ball back. Let's give it a bit, then we'll sneak out and get it." I was battling scenarios of the soldiers coming back and destroying our fence, or worse, our garden. Suddenly, another shriek vibrated through the house. We both jumped at the sound. Although I knew it was probably the mouse, the angry Neighwah and the stolen art shelf had me on edge with weeds twisting their noxious roots through my mind.

"We're caught up on work, so what do you want to do with the rest of our free time? Hey, you know what we should do? We should build a mousetrap." Hayden's excitement and ideas were contagious. Thank heaven, whatever that is, for Hayden; I have a new distraction.

"A grand slam idea," I replied genuinely. "I've heard of putting food at the end of a board, propped up, that hangs over a bucket. When the mouse climbs out on the stick to get the food, the stick gives way and the mouse falls into the bucket and can't get out."

"Cool, let's try it. We're pretty caught up on chores, so let's gather what we need."

I grabbed a weed bucket from the garden. I considered the irony of how a project to trap a mouse just trying to survive could help me with my worry weeds about not getting caught in a trap myself. It took us a couple of tries to get the board to balance enough for a mouse to crawl on it, without it falling too fast. We set it in a corner of the kitchen. Tomorrow, or sooner, we'd see if it worked.

"How did you learn to build stuff like this? Was it from your grandad?" Hayden never called my grandad by the nickname I gave him. He only used it to refer to his lessons. He seemed to know it was a thing between Grandad and me, and he didn't cross that line.

"I saw my dad and GD do this. I don't remember if it worked. I was pretty young."

Meeting Hayden has changed my life. We had only known each other for a few weeks, but I felt close to him. I trusted him, and these secrets were pushing at the seams in my head. I was dying to tell him about some of the forbidden issues I was dealing with. Maybe if I told a seemingly harmless one, it would help me keep the dangerous ones. "My dad and GD taught me some science stuff, especially GD." Let's see how he reacts to that.

"My dad did too, but he said never to tell anyone." Hayden looked around when he said it.

Score! "Did he tell you about the meteorites?" How much does he already know, I wondered.

"He said rocks, called meteorites, fell from the sky when he was too little to remember it. It burned up a lot of stuff and made people sick. Lots and lots of people died."

"That's what I learned, too." I learned so much more, but let's take it slow. "I guess they fell everywhere, and they left craters all over the Earth."

"What's a crater?" Hayden asked.

Okay, so he knew *of* meteorites, but not much *about* meteorites. I wondered how much I should fill in for him. Maybe I could tell him just enough to bait him into our next adventure. "When a meteorite falls through the air, it gets really hot and it burns. Most burn up before they hit the ground, and we call them falling stars. But if it hits the ground, it's going so fast that it gets hot and starts fires, and it also throws up a lot of dirt and leaves a pit called a crater. I've never seen any craters around here, but if we look for one, maybe we could find a meteorite."

"We should totally do that!"

That was too easy, I thought. Now for convincing my dad. I have always wanted to go on a meteorite dig. Lots of people think craters are cursed, so they stay away from them. "We'd have to do it in secret. I don't think my dad would be okay with us making trouble with the superstitious crazies." Some of the crazies are Uppers, and they tend to like telling on Dailys.

"Deal," Hayden said, and we shook. "Now, how to get away with it. That's not easy."

"Well, we are kind of growing out of our little yard. I could tell my dad it's better than hitting soldiers with fly balls." We both laughed. "But seriously, he knows I know how to get to the old ball field. Maybe he'd let us go next week."

"That would be awesome! What would a meteorite look like?" Hayden asked.

I thought about that for a minute. It was a good question, one I had never asked. I know they get hot and burn in the air before they hit. "I think they would look burned or melted. I'm not sure though."

"Okay, catch a mouse and a falling star," and he put his hand up with his palm facing me. I stood there for a moment, not knowing what he was doing, and he finally said, "You're supposed to slap my hand. My dad calls it a high five."

"Cool, I like that," and I slapped his hand.

CHAPTER ELEVEN

The friendship between Hayden and me was growing strong and fast. I wanted desperately to unburden my secrets, but I knew it was wrong to implicate him. But the castle puzzle seemed like a safe endeavor to share. It's just a puzzle, and GD had displayed it in the open, so it can't be that covert.

"I want to show you something my grandad made. I sneaked it out of his room before my mom and dad cleaned it out. They don't know about it, so you can't tell anyone."

"You're the best friend I ever had. I'd never tell on you."

"You know, I wasn't all that excited when my dad told me about you guys coming here, but it's the best thing that ever happened to me." I got down and crawled under my bed where I stashed it. I wasn't about to share the other secrets in the shelf compartment. I pulled it out and unwrapped it from a used-up shirt.

"Wow, that's awesome! Look at the detail of the bricks and the chained bridge." Hayden was entranced by the object.

"It's called a drawbridge. My favorite part is the sword sticking out of the boulder."

"Yeah," Hayden said tilting his head to study it further. "What's up with that? Who stabs a stone?"

"It's from an old story. It could only be pulled out by the rightful king." The story of Camelot was my favorite tale, and I asked GD to tell it to me over and over. "In the story, a poor kid, named Arthur, is the only one who can pull the sword out and become the king. He built a great round table where he and his twelve best knights shared ideas face to face. They were called the Knights of the Round Table."

"I think I'd like that story. Imagine us pulling the sword out, and *BAM*, no one can push us around anymore. He stood holding his imaginary sword aloft, "Give me your allegiance, Knights of the Round Table!"

My mind clicked. The knights' creed, that's it. Be brave, true, wise, gracious, and skilled. It had to be the clue to unlocking the bridge. I needed time to think it through, to try it out, so I just kept quiet.

It was turning out to be a sizzling hot summer, and pumping enough water from the garden tank to keep the garden alive was a huge chore. The territory provided water they pumped through an old pipe system that ran underground. Every day we get an allotted amount, and when we reach the limit, it shuts off until the next day.

Long ago, GD buried a huge tank to supplement water for his garden. He used to fill it with city water, but when they restricted how much we could have, we began filling it before we went to bed until it shut off. We have twenty or more buckets that we used to collect water. If the tank isn't full, we collect rainwater and even snow to pour into that tank for the dry summers. The Corporates don't care if we grow some food for our family. What you could not do was make extra to sell. We hide our garden, but not from the Corporates or Neighwah; we hide it from the desperates and the Drangers. The pump is hidden in an old, cracked plastic trash can.

Dad and I were in the backyard pouring the needed amount of water on each plant using pitchers from the kitchen. We didn't grow the vegetables in rows because scattered plants looked like weeds to those who didn't grow gardens. We hoped the Neighwah soldiers hadn't noticed our garden, and they were focused on finding rock throwers. But the plants were big enough now, and we didn't want trouble from soldiers or thieves.

Hayden would be here soon with his crew, and I needed to talk to my dad about the shelf thing.

I used a low whisper to ask him. "So, Dad, what's going on with the whole thing I found?"

"It's taken care of," he whispered back. "We can't talk about this. Maybe someday, somewhere else, not here."

"What?" I asked in a louder whisper than I meant to.

He returned my question with a stern look and went back to pumping more water into his bucket. That started my mind worrying in a whole new direction. When and where would this conversation ever be okay? Is he talking about when I'm older, or when we aren't here? Where else would we be?

That made me think about my future. How long would Mesh and I live here? Would we have arranged marriages and families? Being older and here in such a full house suddenly made me lose my gumption. Gumption was another GDism. Grandad said it meant having spirited initiative and resourcefulness. I wondered how much gumption I'd have at "somewhere else." What if it's worse? Stupid weeds!

"Hey Dad, that yard is getting too small for us, and we want to start using that bat to hit the ball." He stopped and turned around. I figured he knew what had happened, but he didn't punish me for it. I assumed it was because he understood it was an accident while playing a game he had set up. I had his attention, though. Okay, that was a fast pitch, now for a nice slow changeup.

"I was wondering, can Hayden and I go to the ball field to play today?" His expression said he didn't particularly like the idea, but he was considering it.

"I don't know, Connor. Let me think on it." He was trying to keep his family safe in a forsaken land. He looked like a man with the world on his shoulders. And he was. I bet the worry weeds in his garden are out of control, and I just added to them.

I felt bad for him, but I've been raised on the idea of joy. I have a taste for it, and life without joy is not a life. I needed baseball time with the friend he insisted I have. I needed my castle, art books, and my dragon drawing time. It was easier to live without these things when I was unaware of their effect, but I don't know how to deny myself now.

For a moment, I felt emboldened and willing to fight for these things, but I flashed on the beating my dad took after the garage incident. I realized he would be the one to endure the attack while we watched helplessly on the sidelines. I wish I had never learned about freedom because I yearned for it deeply. This world takes what you love and holds it hostage with a promise that will never come true. Freedom is an impossible dream born in a land of make-believe and wishes. It probably never existed at all. Because if it had, people would never have let it go.

Hayden arrived, and I had to break the news that we still hadn't caught the mouse. We had been trying for four nights now. We stood staring at the bucket, wishing a mouse would appear. My dad walked up behind us.

"What is that contraption you've got there?" My dad looked intrigued, and a spark twinkled in his eye. He was interested in our task and full of gumption himself. I was happy we had given him a momentary reprieve from his parental duties.

"We're trying to catch a mouse. It's been running around the house and making the girls screech." Hayden offered.

"Well, let me see here. What are you using for bait?" Dad asked.

"I didn't want to use anything we needed, so I just put a little flour on the stick," I added.

"Ahhh, that's the problem. It needs to be a little stinky. If a mouse can't smell it, it won't care to check it out." He went to the food box and grabbed the brown clay pot where we kept the cheese my mom made with powdered milk and vinegar. It has been warm lately, so she didn't make very much because it molded quickly. "Here, let's cut off a bit of the moldy part," he said as he balanced it on the thin board, "and we'll see what we catch when we get back."

"Thanks, Dad. Wait, back from where?"

"I thought we could all walk over to the ball field. We'll bring the wagon for Dace."

"Sweet!" Even though I knew that meant meteorite hunting was out, maybe my dad could play ball with us. We hid the bat, gloves, and ball in the wagon under the blanket Dace sat on. Luckily, no one stopped us along the way because a bat could be considered a weapon. I guess even he believes in taking risks for a piece of happiness. The overgrown field was in one of the most damaged and run-down neighborhoods. The cursed houses in the distance were completely abandoned looking wilted with neglect. I guess there was no need to patrol where no one dared to go.

It was a great day. My dad played ball, and he was surprisingly good. He may not have his aim down, but he can throw it far and hard. Dace ran around the field and even threw the ball a time or two. The girls played for a while, but then they sat on a blanket and played with the homemade straw dolls Maylee made with her husband's old clothing. We never saw a single person, and my dad said maybe it would be okay for us to come on our own next time, but we couldn't bring the bat. There were plenty of sticks to be found around the cursed houses, I thought, but I wouldn't let him know that. He had enough weeds to manage.

I was awakened by a bad dream about the shelf and wondered why I didn't dream of dragons anymore. I was trying to fall back to sleep when I heard my mom and dad hush talking in the kitchen.

"How can we just...," I couldn't make out all of what she said, but she continued the next part a little louder, "up into the mountains? The winter will be ... and ... warm *here*," much of what she said was inaudible.

"Shhh, we won't be...," my dad's voice got too quiet for me to hear, so I sat up and listened at the end of my bed near the door.

"What if it's a trap, and...," my dad cut my mom off.

"Shhh, I think I heard something." I quickly and quietly crawled back to the head of my bed and closed my eyes. I heard my dad come down the hall and stop at my open door. I must have fooled him because he went back to the table. I quietly sat back up.

"This is our shot, Rhin." He was whispering loud enough for me to hear now. "It's the only way out. Your dad set it up, and I trust him."

"I thought you said that stupid group was a trick to catch Dailys. You and he went to that weird lecture a month before he... died, but you said that guy just rattled on about how the world *should* be. Dad didn't or wouldn't give us any additional information. He either didn't know, or it was too dangerous to tell you." She was starting to cry because I heard her sniffling while her voice got higher.

"He did give it to me, Rhin. He didn't want you involved. Trust him; trust me." I could hear shuffling, and I assumed he went to hold her.

My head was swirling. Which mountains? We're already in the mountains. Who's leaving? Are we leaving? Are they leaving? Are they running because of the art? Maybe we're taking it somewhere. Maybe we're all leaving! Where, what group? GD, what have you got us into?

CHAPTER TWELVE

Friday came, and I was focusing on work without talking much. I expected Hayden to ask me why, or at least talk about the fun day we had yesterday at the field, but he was kind of quiet too.

"Yesterday was cool, huh?" I said finding the silence too awkward.

"Yeah, it was a blast." Hayden didn't sound very enthusiastic. In fact, he was acting even moodier than me.

"Something wrong, Hays?" I asked, calling him by the nickname I had come up with.

"Just stuff, Condorman," he said, smiling at the new variation on my name.

I guess those are going to stick. I was just about to pump water into the pan to heat it when something caught my eye. "Hays, I think we got a mouse!"

Hayden ran over, and we looked in at the little creature cowering on the edge of the bucket. Hayden looked down at the long-awaited prize with pity. "He has it even worse than we do. Let's throw it over the fence into our field. It's far enough that it won't come back here."

"Then it will get into someone else's house and make a mess."

"Yeah, well, today I just don't feel like killing it. It's bad enough it will lose its home." Hayden said, and I swallowed hard at the difficult subject. I studied Hayden when he finally looked up at me, and he studied me too. I felt him look right into my mind and all the weeds it grew there. We went into the yard, climbed through the fence to our mini-field, and dumped the mouse out into the next vacant yard. We watched it scurry away and under a bush. We stood there looking deeply into the tiny field. I stared at that bush, letting my mind wander.

Hayden turned and sadly confessed his secret. "I'm not supposed to tell you, but my dad is being transferred to a different part of the territory. We're starting to pack up and choose what we have to leave behind."

I was stunned. I can't lose my best friend again. I thought about what I heard last night, but I had no idea what it meant, so I said nothing. "Do you know where you're going?"

He shook his head. "We were given a list of stuff to pack, but I heard my stepmom say the list doesn't make sense. When I asked to see it, my dad put it in his pocket. Later that night, when they finished putting all the stuff for packing in their room, he threw it in the wood stove and burned it."

I was dying to tell him about the conversation I overheard last night, but I had no idea what it meant, or if it was connected to the stolen art. Even though I trust him, I just can't endanger him with that.

"What I don't understand is why my parents are being so secretive. I mean, if the Corporates are moving us, why can't we talk about it?" We looked at each other while shadows and secrets danced inside us. We both knew it, like we both knew such things must stay in darkness.

"You know, my parents have also been doing a lot of whispering lately. They make sure I can't hear them clearly, so I don't know what they were talking about." Not a complete lie, I thought. "I wish we knew what was going on." I wish we could talk honestly about what we knew.

"They should tell us. They should trust us." Hayden's last words were so fizzled out that it was close to an omission.

I hated the awkward distance between us. I hated the reality that *we* couldn't even trust each other.

By the time Thursday came, my dad decided to let us go to the ball field on our own. We weren't sure how many Thursdays we had left. Maybe this was the last one. On the way, Hayden told me soldiers in full gear and dark helmets had picked up the boxes they had packed.

"It was kind of scary," he said. "They never said a word, and they made my dad sign some agreement thing. We were in the first bedroom, peeking down the hall. Dace didn't cry, but he held on to my leg awful tight until they left. All my dad would say is, 'Trust me.'" Hayden rolled his eyes.

"Yeah, I'm pretty sick of the just trust me thing too. We have to trust them, but they don't trust us."

Hayden nodded at my statement while standing with his arms crossed in front of him.

I was dying to tell him about the no-kitchen house designs, but that could get him in trouble too. I felt bad that I had so many secrets from him, but they were just too dangerous. Maybe our moving thing had to do with that. Maybe my dad told his dad about it. No, I didn't believe that. My dad is too cautious.

We walked over to the empty houses we were warned to stay away from, to find a stick to use as a bat. It was creepy walking down the street through the sagging houses. Some were caved in, some scorched by an ancient fire, and almost every window was removed or broken.

"Hayden, have you ever heard of dragons?" I couldn't say anything about the art or the sliding shelf, but maybe dragons are not an uncommon myth animal.

"You know, I recently heard Maylee tell Dace and Savannah a bedtime story about a dragon. A dangerous, giant, flying lizard that breathes fire. They are magical creatures that steal and hoard gold. It was a cool story."

"They have gold! I never read about that." I knew it the minute I said the word *read,* it was a mistake. Now he knows I have a book on them. He knows I have a stash of books under my floorboards, but I can't share that book with him. It has a lot of art in it. Probably the same pilfered art squatting in my room, just waiting to be outed by stupid mistakes, like this.

"You read about them? Where did you read about dragons?"

I was trying to come up with a lie, but I just wasn't thinking fast enough. He saw my look of alarm and half frowned at me. "It's okay. I can tell you said something you regret. It's a time of secrets. I have them too. They feel like carrying a load of bricks everywhere I go, very heavy."

"You know, Hays, if I could tell anyone my secrets, it would be you. I just don't want you to be punished for my troubles."

"I get it, Condorman. I do." He looked forward like he was seeing miles into the distance without focusing on anything.

We walked a while, letting the silence drown our disposition, but it didn't last long. It couldn't, not when we were together.

"Hey, do you think any meteorites fell here?" Hayden asked, breaking our sullen mood.

"Maybe, let's look at that row of burned-up houses."

We searched the area, but it was just a heap of charred debris. There was a large, round dip in the ground that had been used as a dump. If a meteorite did hit here, it was covered with tons of twisted, jagged, and charred junk. We didn't go near the mess. It would be just our luck to bleed out from a cut or get sick. But we did find two black rocks.

"I don't know, Hays. I kinda doubt they're meteorites. Maybe they're dragon rocks," I said, laughing.

Hayden looked down at his dark rock as if it were precious. "Maybe they aren't meteorites, maybe they are, but whenever I see this or any black rock, I'll remember this day."

We each had one as a way to remember each other, and we decided to deem them meteorites.

"HEY!" someone yelled.

We both jumped and dashed between two houses. Peeking around the corner, we saw an old man dressed in the worst rags I had ever seen. They seemed to drip off his body in numerous tears.

"You two," he continued yelling, "RUN! They're coming, I tell you! The nukes are coming!" He was dramatically waving his arms with a wild look in his eyes.

We stepped out from behind the house.

"What are nukes?" shouted Hayden.

I couldn't believe he was talking to this guy. I gave him the wide-eyed, *he-could-be-dangerous* look.

"They are the meteorites men make," he yelled. He looked out of his mind, insane. He was probably a toxer—someone who poisons their body with toxins found at dump sites to escape the world.

Or maybe there really was a curse.

"And they're coming. Coming to end us all. Get away from here! Go!"

We ran all the way home. I wanted to ask my dad about the old man and nukes, but we weren't supposed to go near the houses. Dad had secrets from me, I had secrets from him, and we both had secrets from Mom. I have secrets from Hayden, as he does from me. How did everything get so complicated?

Before Hayden left that evening, I gave him the ball glove he had been using. It was a good thing I did, because he was gone the next morning. I knew he was going to move, but why wasn't he allowed to say goodbye? I felt profoundly sad. This was the worst year of my life. Everything I loved in my life kept slipping away. First Grandad, now Hayden, and something was coming next, but I didn't know what.

Hayden had been gone for three weeks, and I had been working on the castle. I used the knight's creed as my guide. Be brave was the first vow, and I remembered how the bridge poked me. Maybe like, B for brave and bridge. I grabbed the top of the bridge and pushed the pin tucked behind it with a pencil. Nothing. Well, using a pencil wasn't very brave, so I used my finger. I braced myself for the stab and inserted my finger in the divot. I pushed through my body's alert, and the bridge opened a little and stopped. There was just enough room for the rest of my finger. Nice GD, your own little torture chamber. Taking a breath, I pushed deeper. Something gripped my finger with little spikes that would rip my skin if I pulled it out. I kept pushing, and *click*, the bridge released. I pulled the drawbridge down; the medieval gripping device moved back to the sides, releasing my finger.

The inside was painted rather simply, and nothing was stored in it. The only detailed design was a compass painted on the floor. It took me several days to make the connection to the next clue—be true. It dawned on me when my dad was talking about a northbound road he would be working on the next day. Of course, true north. GD was always talking about constantly needing to reset one's moral compass. But how could I do that with a castle? What starts with T? Towers! Sure enough, the tallest tower could rotate. One stone turret had a crested banner painted on it, so I turned it north according to the compass on the floor. No clue appeared to help me with the next step. The next vow was to be wise, and beyond the guess it had to do with a window or the water in the mote, it had me stumped. Again, I set it back under my bed for later.

Then it happened.

My dad broke the news that *we* would be moving, but we couldn't tell anyone.

Of course, I had questions, but they were all answered with non-answers.

When I asked him where we were going, he said *somewhere else*. When will we move? *Sometime soon.* Why? *It's a work thing.* What will our new home be like? *Whatever they give us.*

Finally, my attitude kicked in, "So Dad, how will we get to somewhere else, sometime soon, to live in whatever they give us, for the work thing? I guess the answer to that is somehow." I hoped he would see how crazy his answers had been. I was mad, so I didn't care if it made him mad. He just started laughing.

"It's more organized than it seems. Changes like this cause security issues for the Neighwah if everyone is talking about it. Just lie low, don't tell anyone, and do as your mom and I say," he sighed. "Connor, you're just going to have to trust me." *Trust you, oh yeah, like I didn't see that coming.*

Two days later, four big wooden boxes plus two small ones were dropped off at our house. It was on my mom's day off. She just opened the door and let the two soldiers into our house. Their black uniforms had lots of zippered pockets and straps that held equipment and ammo. A holster on each side held black weapons, and another long gun was slung over their shoulders. The black helmets had a wide reflective visor, allowing complete peripheral vision. Hayden had described them, so I wasn't surprised, but I was definitely intimidated. It wouldn't be long now, and we would disappear like Hayden and his family.

Maybe that's what happens to the missing. Maybe they know about the art shelf, and we're going to end up buried somewhere else.

My dad barely got inside the door. "Dad, I need to talk to you, man to man."

"Okay, just let me put my stuff down." He looked over and saw the boxes. "Oh, good," he said, "we can start packing."

"Dad!" I was trying so hard not to scream. "I don't want to leave GD's house. I don't want to get rid of all of our stuff. I'm tired of secrets and changes and losing people I love." My emotions came pouring out. I couldn't control it. My dad brought me to my room.

"Connor, you have every right to be upset. It's been crazy for me too. Okay, what I'm going to tell you is as secret as the shelf."

I looked at my dad with my red-rimmed eyes. "I've never said a word to anyone about that, Dad, not even Hayden. On my honor, I haven't. You can trust me."

"I believe you. You've had a lot on your young shoulders, and I'm proud of how you've carried it, and how you've helped out around here without complaining. We are joining a group of people. They are trying to make a fair and better place to live . This is very dangerous stuff. We could all be killed, tortured, and made to tell what we know so everyone gets caught. Do you see how serious this is? This group is also who GD kept the art hidden for, so they are going to take it along with our boxes. That is all I can say. It's not much better than somewhere else, someday, or somehow, but just let this play out, and don't go snooping around. It could bring everything down on us. Okay?"

"It seems too much to get away with. It scares me. Life isn't great here, but I know it, but I'm used to it. Why can't we just stay?"

"Things are not going to get better," my dad had a weary look. "They say worse times are coming."

"You mean because of the nukes?" I knew I might get in trouble, but maybe that old man wasn't so nuts after all.

"Where did you hear that word? Do you know what a nuke is?" He was stunned.

"We saw an old man when we went to check the cursed houses for meteorites."

"Oh, Connor," my dad sighed to himself, "so dangerous."

"He was yelling about the nukes coming and ending us all. Hayden asked him what a nuke was, and he said it was the meteorites that men made."

"Well," he said and paused, "I guess that is as good a description as any. They do the same kind of damage, but nukes, short for nuclear weapons, also give off a poison. He probably *is* just a ranting old man. I haven't heard anything about nukes."

"Hey Dad, could you tell me one more thing? Do you know where Hayden went? Please don't lie or give me some non-answer." I went on to describe the soldiers who came to Hayden's house. "And then they just disappeared. Hayden would have told me goodbye, so they didn't let him."

"Connor, on my honor, I don't know, but it sounds possible they may have joined the same group from your description of events."

He hugged me, and I believed in him, and it made me feel safe again. I don't know why I believed he could keep me protected in such a dangerous world. He was only one man, but so far, he had. I didn't understand exactly what he meant by a fair place to live, but I was clinging to the hope that I'd see Hayden again, and maybe soon.

CHAPTER THIRTEEN

I was not included in packing the house. I wasn't even included in packing my stuff. I didn't own many things, so I was able to figure out what she took. Oddly enough, the stuff I used the most was still in my dresser.

I came into the kitchen one evening and stood in front of my mom. I was holding up my glove, ball, bat, and chalkboard for her to see. "Are we not taking these things?" I asked, my voice saturated with a heated temper.

"Those things will travel with us, don't worry," my mom answered sweetly.

She had a kind heart, and it was hard to be mad at her sometimes, but I was mad this time. "What's the point of splitting our stuff up? Why don't we just take it all at once? Why did you alter the someday clothes from the attic to fit me? Why didn't you take any of the work clothes I actually wear?"

"We won't have enough room to take everything. We have to prioritize."

It suddenly occurred to me. "Is Dad being promoted? Is he going to work with the Uppers? Is that why we need nicer clothes? Are we just going to leave our garden, our furniture, and everything we have that we know keeps us fed and warm?"

"Connor! Settle down!" My dad entered the room.

Good, here's someone I can fight with. "Dad, seriously, you weren't here when those soldiers came into *our house*. They were drenched in guns and ammo. If they aren't Neighwah, they're still bad-a…"

"Watch your mouth, young man!" His jaw was tensed as he stepped toward me. I froze. My mom stood behind me. Pickle in the middle, and I was the pickle with no safe base to run to. Done, out. I have never seen him turn that much anger my way. He suddenly looked a lot bigger. I turned and sulked back to my bedroom like a batter doing a shame walk to the dugout.

I sat on my bed, GD's bed. Everything in here reminded me of him. He surrounded me, comforted me. It helped me remember. All the memories we shared were built into this house. His desk was robbed of all his work, and soon the hidden shelf would be empty too. He risked his life for that art, if that's even what it is. I only got to see one thing, and that one thing left me spellbound. What if I never get to see the dragon again or the rest of it? It was so important GD risked us all, and I'll never even know what it was. And what was I supposed to do with the art books and the castle? How would I transport it to this somewhere else place? Would I have to confess I broke into GD's room after being told not to? I felt the weeds twisting and tightening around my throat, and I was having trouble breathing.

I was lying down on my bed when Mesh came in.

"Connor, are you sad to leave?" Her lost look mirrored my own, and she was coming to me for comfort and courage. I can only imagine how confused she is, but she still has that blind faith that Mom and Dad will protect her. I have faith they'll try, but I also know they could fail, especially with the choices they were making. I seemed to gather myself and my courage for her. She needed me, and I needed to step up.

"Yeah, I'm just saying goodbye. But I'm excited too. We get to go on an adventure and ride in a vehicle!" I must have convinced her because she smiled and crawled up to sit with me. "It's going to be cool, you'll see." I was pretty sure I'd have to backtrack that lie later, but it was working for now. It's the same thing my parents were doing to me. Lying to make me feel safe, but it wasn't working.

"Tell me an adventure story," she asked, "like what it will be like." I had no clue what it would be like, but I used the stories from GD to create a wonderful world of happiness. I was pretty proud of it, and I thought it was one of my best stories. I looked down at Mesh, and she was curled under my arm, sound asleep.

The soldiers came back two days later when it was my dad's day off. It was an hour after the shift horn had blown, and two hours before the ration lines would open. The streets were empty, and most people were working at their jobs or in their homes. No one would question the fiercely dressed soldiers. I wondered if he would realize his folly and react differently when the fully armed soldiers walked into our home, but he just quietly told us to go to Meshka's room, and he let them in.

The door to her room was closed, but I remembered that mouse hole with a view to the entrance between the kitchen and front room area. I got down, cleared it out, and peered through it. All I could see were their boots at floor level near the wall that bordered the front room. They were using a drill to remove screws, and then I saw the edge of a hatch flip up. I saw the soldiers as they climbed down, and I worried they might see the hole I was using. But they were very focused and came back up carrying long, flat wooden crates.

Two by two they loaded them onto the hand trucks and wheeled them out. On the third run, one rolled off, and the contents spilled open. I almost screamed from shock when it hit the floor and slid right next to the mouse hole. The label read "ammunition." When the one near me was picked up, I could see lots of them. My heart caught in my throat. I began to imagine what the other boxes held. What the heck, GD! Were you preparing for a war? Those must have been the last two boxes because one soldier began to screw the hatch back down while the other collected the boxes back into the crate and wheeled them out of my sight.

Next was my room. I assumed from the rumbling sound that they were collecting the art. I had my ear to the wall with the shelf that was between our rooms. Meshka was looking at me, but not saying a word. She seemed to understand it was a secret, and she was quiet. The slide of the shelf was followed by more shuffling. I could hear my dad's muffled voice, but I don't think the soldiers spoke one word. It was quickly emptied, and the shelf rolled back into place. I still had my ear to the wall when I heard footsteps at the door. I turned and whispered to Mesh, "Shhh," and stepped back.

"You can come out now," my dad said.

"I didn't know we were done packing." I went around opening the kitchen cabinets. "There's hardly anything gone from the kitchen."

"Connor, stop! I swear to you, everything is going as planned. Don't scare your sister."

"We'll be taking some stuff in the van with us. We aren't leaving for another week. Those things were sent ahead and will be at our place when we get there," my dad said in a shaky voice that strove to be seen as calm and logical. It was apparent that the event had rattled him too.

He turned his head to busy himself with drying off the counter, mumbling, "Yeah, it will be waiting."

He didn't sound too convinced, but I agreed we shouldn't argue with Mesh around. "Who will live here when we're gone? Can we ever come back?"

"A family your mom knows from work just had twin girls. They were living near here with his parents and younger sister, but there isn't enough room for them now. Your mom is leaving a box of old clothes for them, so they could cut them up for baby clothes and diapers. We're leaving them several other things too. With the garden and the special additions in this house, they'll have a better life than they would in a new renter house.

"Oh, well, that's nice that *they* will have a better life," I said sarcastically. "What about us? It took years for Grandad to make this place safe, and we've worked hard to build up those supplies. It looks like we're going to starve and freeze at this somewhere else."

"No," my dad said. "We're transfers. We'll get a nicer place, a step up. But Connor, we're going to have to leave the baseball bat. We can't transport a weapon. I'm sorry. I'll make you a new one."

As I turned to sulk back to my room. I stopped where the hatch was now covered with a rug. Yeah, keeping my bat weapon is out of the question, but guns and ammo are perfectly fine though. What other stuff besides arms, wood, and food was kept down there? How long had that been there? How big is it? It was probably where they sheltered during the meteorite storm. I sighed as I stepped into my room.

The desk was gone! They knew what that desk meant to me, and they sent it off without telling me. It's probably the only way they could get it to "somewhere else." I decided not to ask. I just wouldn't talk to them. Let them wonder. Let their weeds grow for a while. It gave me some satisfaction, the vengeful kind.

CHAPTER FOURTEEN

It was less than a week later when the van pulled up in front of our house. My mom wasn't kidding about leaving stuff for the new family. The garden was bursting with a promising harvest that was barely a month away. We took everything we could, but left the rest. My mom took a few jars of canned food from last fall but left all the canning supplies she bought with our precious credits. She did pack all of our food and her favorite pan, but that was it from the kitchen. She left GD's precious cast-iron pans. I stared at the hand-washer for clothes. It was unpacked too. As much as I hated that thing, it would be a lot more work without it. At least she was smart enough to bring some of our blankets.

How will we live without our kitchen stuff? Suddenly, I remembered those house plans without kitchens. But where will we store or cook food? How could it possibly work? Perhaps our rations would be prepared at a community kitchen. I imagined miserable walks in bad weather. Maybe my parents sold the artwork and weapon supplies. They would certainly be valuable enough to change our status if we could get away with it. But maybe my dad did have a working plan, and we were going to get all new stuff. Now, that was the first thing that made any sense. I liked that theory, and it seemed to be the only reasonable conclusion. The alternative was that my parents had lost their minds.

I grabbed my art supplies, the art book, and the castle from the shelf compartment. I stuffed the book and art supplies into the bottom of my tote. I wrapped the castle carefully with an old shirt and tied my extra pair of shoes and my grow-into pair in a circle around it, and then I wrapped it in my jacket and put it in my ample tote. It's not that the castle itself was illegal, but why a Daily had such a nice item could cause issues and most probably end with its confiscation. My weeds were growing out of control as I handed mine and Meshka's totes to the driver standing at the back of the van. He put them in a large space behind the rows of torn and dirty seats. My dad and mom gave the man their packed totes and three medium-sized boxes of belongings to go in the back. I felt a little better when he piled their two soft totes on top of ours.

I helped Mesh take a seat behind the driver, and I took the one next to her with a full view out the front windshield and a side window too. I had ridden in the back of a truck once when I was registered as a nine-year-old. But I hadn't ridden inside one, and I wanted to see everything on this road trip. I didn't know what to do with the straps and buckles draped on the seats, so I pushed them to the edge. When my mom got in, she buckled the strap around me and then around Mesh.

"Is the ride so rough that we have to be strapped in?" I asked innocently.

"No, it's only in case we hit something and have an accident. Don't worry."

It's in case we have an accident and crash, is what I heard. I'm tired of people saying don't worry, and every time they do, I worry more. The van door closed, and we moved forward on the bumpy street. I was looking out the front and the side windows at our neighborhood. I turned and watched GD's house, the only home I had ever known, fade in the distance. I felt a deep ache of tragic sadness well up in my core. I closed my eyes, not able to watch it fade away forever.

We headed toward central Denver. Before we hit downtown, we stopped at two more houses. Four more people got in, and all the empty seats behind us were filled. I felt more at ease as more items buried my stolen art book and precious castle. No one talked much, but now and again, someone would point out something and throw out unimportant statements. I recognized the "I-have-a-secret" manner of conversation. I guess everyone battles worry weeds.

The houses were in better shape toward the center of town. The Uppers lived here in their nice neighborhoods, but scattered to the edges were the Dailys' homes. The contrast was brazen and insensitive. The structures became sparser, and the shabbiness of the houses became worse the further from the town center we went. When the last structures faded away, the road made a straight line toward the mountains. The van creaked and squeaked along the pitted highway as the terrain spread out into a wide-open sea of wild land. We sailed through it mile after mile. It was hypnotizing.

Mesh had fallen asleep against me. Though I was tired, I fought the heavy pull of sleep to take in the scenery. I'd never seen so much land. It seemed to go on forever without buildings claiming it. A truck passed us going the other way, and it struck me it was the first vehicle we had seen since leaving town. I guess there are not many travelers this far out. Where were we going? What would it be like? I could feel the weeds taking back over.

We were in the middle of nowhere. No sign of civilization could be seen. This trust thing was working on my sanity. All of a sudden, I saw it, and I was thrilled beyond measure. A deep gash ran along the mountainside in the shape of a long teardrop. I imagined Vadina flying swiftly over the crags and peaks, firing her powerful flame across the mountainside while surveying the endless open land.

I wondered if Hayden had seen the meteor scorch mark on his journey. I pointed it out to my dad, and he raised his eyebrows and nodded his head.

At that moment, it felt like I had cleared a whole area of worry weeds. Being excited, focused, and confident was the cure for my moody garden. That was my own "ism." I couldn't wait to tell Hayden, and I'm determined and focused on seeing him again. More weeds gone. I could feel my body relaxing and my confidence shining through the clouds of doubt as they parted.

"How long have we been driving?" I asked my dad.

"It's been just over an hour since we left our house. We're more than halfway now," he said.

My thoughts returned to Hayden, and how to go about finding him when we arrived. I was exhausted, and I felt the tug of sleep. I'll just close my eyes for a second.

Meteorites streaked across the night sky with an ominous red glow. Everyone was running while I stood still, my eyes focused on the spectacle. I knew I had to run, but I couldn't take my eyes off the majestic splendor of raw power. Frozen in place, I saw the wild storm of dust and burning wreckage sweep toward me with a vengeance, but I stood my ground unafraid. The next thing I knew, Mesh was pulling me out of my dream and tugging on my sleeve.

"Look," she said and pointed ahead.

In the distance, I saw a small shack-like building. A Neighwah off-road truck and a small car were parked on the side of the road. Our driver slowed as he approached the checkpoint. Why hadn't I been told about this? Why didn't I guess? The soldiers were going through the bags of the people from the small car. Panic hit me, and I felt the familiar strangling weeds tightening their grip on my resolve and obliterating my newfound courage.

The submissive couple ahead of us reloaded their car trunk and pulled out onto the road. It was our turn now. The Neighwah soldier approached the van on the driver's side. The driver rolled the window down.

"Papers," the soldier said unceremoniously. The driver handed him the folder with all the passengers' transfer paperwork.

He thumbed through them and handed them back through the window to the driver. "Open the back and have the passengers step outside."

Stay calm, I said to myself. Don't let them see you flinch. He went through two of the bags on top and opened one of Mom's boxes. The vice grip of fear continued to squeeze my chest, and I thought of the horrible things that would happen to everyone in my company. My guilt was crushing me. I was to blame for this, and if the book was found, it would scar us all forever. Grandad, what have I done? I wish you were here with me. The soldier grabbed another bag, still not mine, and began to search it. Why did I take it, keep it, bring it? I remembered what GD said about focusing on what you want to happen. I had to change my focus. If I didn't focus on a positive result, how could I expect one? I was still undiscovered. I just needed a base hit.

I was counting mountain peaks, locating colors around me, and listing baseball terms in my head. Any task I could think of to keep my thoughts off the castle and especially the art book, because there was little doubt in my mind that it contained a detailed description of the stolen art. They might be unaware of the individual artworks, but the pieces that were stolen from the Denver Museum of Art would be general knowledge to checkpoint soldiers. The very pieces held at our house were the ones illustrated in this special exhibit booklet, of that I was certain.

Controlling my breathing, I watched them get closer and closer to the bottom of the pile where my bag was sitting. Then I saw it. He was pulling it out of the pile. I felt the vines twisting around my chest as my heart pounded in my ears. My breaths came quick and shallow, but no matter how much air I took, suffocating panic set in, and my head began to spin. I wanted to close my eyes to settle my nerves, but my life and the lives of my family dangled along with that handle in the soldier's hand.

It was then a radio call sang out. I could almost make out the garbled voice on the other side saying something about the next shift approaching. The soldier held the handle of my bag, straining the last of my resolve as he listened to the crackly voice on the other end. I kept thinking as hard as I could, *put it back, put it back, please put it back.*

Without any conversation from his team member, he threw the bag back into the van. I breathed out a sigh much too loudly, I thought, but I could feel the shared release of tension among the other passengers as well. Maybe I didn't hold the only secrets, or they worried they were traveling with someone like me. Almost immediately, the soldiers signaled for us to gather our tousled belongings on the road and repack them in the van.

We were all anxious to be on our way before the next shift crew found a reason to keep us. It wasn't until we passed the truck coming to relieve the soldiers behind us that I fully caught my breath. I don't know how I got so lucky, and I promised I would not be so careless again. I tried to get back the confidence the meteorite scar had inspired, but it seemed like a foolish, distant memory I couldn't grasp.

We came to a freshly painted sign nailed to the crooked remnants of a dead tree trunk. The white, hand-painted letters read "Fairplay." Was this my dad's idea of a joke when he said he was trying to get to a fair place to live? Most of the buildings were falling apart like our town, but some of them were brand new. Denver had repaired buildings, but this town had several completely new structures. The fresh wood, new paint, and strong, straight edges had a beauty I had never noticed in a building before. I suddenly had an understanding of Grandad's love of architecture. We pulled up to two houses joined together, and the van stopped.

"Wayther house," said the driver nonchalantly. He got out and walked to the back. We unbuckled our straps and climbed out of the vehicle while the other passengers remained. My legs felt rubbery and weird. We walked to the back and grabbed our gear. I looked at the small duplex. Not bigger, to the disappointment of us all, it was quite a bit smaller than what we had. I guess he didn't sell the art or the weapons.

CHAPTER FIFTEEN

I had seen two-in-one houses like this in Denver. This one, like many, was joined together with matching garages that had chimneys sticking out of them. We gathered our totes and headed up the walk to the front door. My dad had to make a couple of trips from the curb to bring the boxes that hopefully held everything we would need to live up here.

He put the boxes down by the front door, where we all stood anxiously. He reached above the garage door frame and moved along the shallow edge until he found the key. I was checking out the intact picture window next to the front door. I guess we'll hang our clothes in the garage again.

"Okay, moment of truth," he said and opened the door.

I'm not sure what he or any of us expected, but none of us were instantly charmed by it. The front room was painted a light peach and white, and it went well with the brick fireplace. The fireplace had a swing bar for hanging a pot to heat water, and the woodbox was full of split wood. At least we had a heat source and an extra place to heat water. The matching gray chair and couch were worn, but no more than the stuff we left behind. A dark brown coffee table sat in front of the couch, and a shelf was against the opposite wall. It would be useful for things we need to have or remember as we come and go.

From the front room, I could see into the kitchen and the dining room. I half expected the floor plan to look like the ones my grandad drew without kitchens, so why he drew those remains a mystery. It was smaller than our old kitchen, but it had an electric stove, not a wood stove. My dad flicked the light switch just for fun, and a light came on in the kitchen. We had electricity! While he played with the knobs on the stove, I checked the refrigerator. We each turned with a thumbs up; both were working. We soon found out that the electricity was limited to lights and kitchen appliances. And though we still didn't have hot water like the Uppers, it was a major step up, and it was going to change everything.

Rows of open shelves above, and cupboards below contained several kinds of pans and dishes. I checked the bins for flour, rice, and oatmeal, and they were full! I found enough utensils for eating and cooking in a drawer by the deep double sink. The water pump worked, and upon my first couple of cranks, a strong stream of clear water poured out of the spout. The broom closet had a mop, a bucket, a broom, and a dustpan.

The counter was empty, making it look quite spacious. A painted food locker stood against the wall with a pressure latch on the side to keep out vermin. In what used to be a laundry room, a hand clothes washer and wringer complete with wash tubs nestled against the wall. Beyond that room was the door to the garage. A table with four chairs faced a big glass door to the backyard. I pulled the curtains aside and saw there was no fence, and it was covered in tall, stubborn weeds. It made me laugh inside at the irony. Too late to plant a garden anyway.

Between the kitchen and the front room, a large metal box stood on the wall with slits in it. My dad said it was a heater. It was a nice summer day, but I'm sure we'll try it out tonight. If it worked, it was reassuring that we'd have two heat sources to battle the brutal cold this high up. The first door down the hall went to a bathroom. Happily, that water pump worked too. The tub was a typical size and relatively clean for how old it appeared to be. The next door led to a small bedroom. A twin bed was parked across from a bright yellow shelf, and those were the only furnishings in it. It seemed logical that this should be Mesh's room.

The door across the hall led to another bedroom that was about the same size. I immediately set my bag on the bed and felt my way to the bottom, searching for the two books and castle tucked down in there. It was careless to pack them with me. But there they were. I flopped onto the bed, holding my bag to my chest. I have no idea how I made it through that ambush, how we all did. I felt awful about how much danger I put everyone in. Restless from the thoughts in my head, I got up and looked out the window at the overgrown yard we traded for our bountiful garden. My garden of worry weeds was mirrored out that window.

I wished so hard my grandad was here to advise me and save me. I closed my eyes, trying to imagine him here in some form unknown to me. I needed some sort of tangible feeling of him being here with me, protecting me, and teaching me, and then I thought of the call that saved us. "Thanks, GD. I'll be more careful. I promise." I said quietly.

I finally opened my eyes and decided to settle into my new room. I looked around and saw nothing that made me hate it. I will miss GD's queen-sized bed, but the twin was plenty big enough for me. An extra blanket sat on a chair positioned in the corner by the window. The last days of August were still nice, but the nights here are probably quite cold already, and soon it would be miserably cold. I opened the window, and a light breeze carried the sun-faded curtains gently into the room. The air here smelled so fresh, and I drew in its crispness deeply.

I could feel the effects of the elevation, but I knew how to deal with altitude illness and how to avoid it. I looked up at the mountain rising outside. The air was so clear; I swear I could see the needles on the distant trees. They were old, straight, and tall despite setting their roots in the rugged terrain. In Denver, I knew there were mountains, but I never really saw them through the haze. They never rose and demanded my attention like the magnificent sight currently at my window. Okay, I admit, the place has potential.

No dresser was available, but half the closet was for hanging up clothes, and the other half had shelves. I shook them, but they didn't move, and it made me smile. One of the shelves had a door on it. I decided it was the only place to put my art supplies, chalkboard, and sketchbook, but the art book and the castle had to be hidden. I decided to stuff the book under the bottom end of my mattress and the castle under my bed. I emptied the rest of my stuff and started putting it away. I didn't have much, so it wasn't long before I lay down. The bed was more comfortable than GD's, one more point for Fairplay.

I wanted to hate the new house, but it wasn't bad. Nothing in this house was any worse, and having electricity was better than what we had, but it was smaller and missing a garden and a fence. The paint was newer than at our house, but it wasn't freshly painted. The furnishings were just as old as our old stuff, but it was someone else's old stuff. I wanted ours. I remembered the crates we had sent ahead, and I dashed out to the garage. I couldn't wait to see GD's desk. I opened the door. There was a snow shovel, a couple of garden tools, a rickety wagon, a nice pile of logs ready to split, and a splitting maul, but no crates, no desk, no art.

"DAD!," I yelled, rushing back into the house. I ran to the end of the hall to their room where my mom and he were already unpacking their totes. "Dad, our crates aren't here! Grandad's desk isn't here! They took them a week ago. Did they steal them?"

"Connor, look! We're back to two bathrooms," my mom was trying to distract me with random chatter, but it wasn't going to work, and my dad knew it.

"Settle down, Connor. I'll figure it out. They weren't stolen."

"How do you know? What about Grandad's desk? Do you even know what's going on? It looks like you and Mom have given away everything and got this in return. Have you guys gone crazy?"

Mom left the room and closed the door behind her. While my dad guided me to sit on the bed. "Connor, we will get all our stuff. I wish I could tell you when."

"I know you know more than you're telling me," I said with a look of fury.

"True, but think about the shelf. You didn't tell Hayden, and you wouldn't tell Meshka. But you know why you can't tell, right?"

"Yes," I said quietly, but I could see where this was going.

"Then you understand," and I knew that was game over, end of discussion. "Now go and settle into your new room."

There seemed to be more Neighwah in this town. They were everywhere. Our ration day was scheduled for the day after our arrival. It was my mom's day off, and she would have to go alone or take me and Mesh with her. I convinced her to take us. None of us knew this town, and I didn't want her to be harassed. I was thinking of the Drangers when I thought of harassers, but the Neighwah were no less threatening. We passed three Neighwah soldiers in just five blocks of walking. Even though she was my mother, I'd have to be blind not to notice she was stunning. Good-looking women were always a target for jerks.

I was worried about carrying rations when we left our wagon at our old house, but there was one in the garage. I could see it would soon need repairs, but it worked okay for now. I found it strange that we left so much stuff, and even stranger that the family who lived here before did as well. I wondered if any of their stuff had sentimental meanings like ours. We had walked three blocks uphill and had two more to go. I was extraordinarily out of breath for such a short walk, but I knew the nine-thousand-plus altitude was the reason. To take my mind off the labor, I decided to make up a story about our new wagon for Mesh.

"So, Mesh, I have been looking at our new home and the belongings in it, and I figured out something about this wagon," I lied, but not a mean lie, a fun, comforting lie. The kind parents tell kids.

"What?" she asked with blind faith and attentiveness. She shifted the empty ration bins piled in the wagon to look at me.

"Well, I bet someone's dad or grandad made it for the little girl who lived in our house before us."

"How do you know that?" she asked suspiciously.

"You know how your room has a flower painted on the end of the bed? Well, I bet it was a girl's room, maybe she was your age." I was stretching the facts. I would take a bed with ten flowers on it over the cold floor.

"Don't boys like flowers?" she said, crossing her arms while her blue eyes looked straight through me.

These past couple of months have changed her too. "Yeah, I love flowers, but if someone was going to take the time to paint something on my bed, I'd want baseball stuff or meteorites." I regretted it the moment I said it. My mom looked at me with a surprised look. And the question came.

"What are mead-o-rites?" She was in full listening mode.

"It's just what black rocks are called, but it's not a word Dailys should say because it's an angry word, so don't ever say it out loud." Good save, I thought.

"Why would you want black rocks painted on your bed if they mean bad words? What are gray rocks called? Are there blue and green rocks? Or, ooh, yellow rocks. Are there yellow rocks? Do they have names too?" I looked at my mom, and she was holding in her laughter at the quagmire I had stepped into.

"Let's just get back to the story. So, this little girl who lived in your room before you, what do you think she was like? It's just make-believe, but it's fun to pretend." Please let this get back on track. I could feel my lungs laboring with the stress of the last hill. I stopped and leaned on my knees to take a couple of breaths while signaling to my mom that I was fine.

"I think her name was," Mesh paused, "Debbie. She had blonde hair like me, but green eyes like you. And she had four dolls. That's more than anyone has, but we're just pretending." She smiled her infectious smile, and it occurred to me that when she got a little older, she would be a target too.

We got in the ration line, which was shorter than the lines we were used to, but it still stretched along the walkway outside. Meshka was continuing the game further than my interest in it lasted. I was observing the system and the amount of food in the boxes as the people leaving walked by. I scanned each person remotely fitting the description of Hayden or anyone from his family, but no luck. Although this was the only ration station in town, it was unlikely we would be assigned the same day. Heck, I didn't even know what town he moved to, but it was too soon to give up hope.

We were almost at the front door. Mesh was tugging on my sleeve, and it interrupted my surveillance. She motioned me to bend down. "Look," she whispered in my ear. "Are those mead-o-rites?"

I looked down, and off the path was a pile of black rocks. It was odd that they were sitting there in an unnatural pile. I picked them up but none of them were Hayden's. My mind began to race. Was it a message from Hayden? Why would he leave a message here? He didn't know I was moving. I didn't even find out until after he was gone. Mesh was tugging on me, awaiting the answer to her clever question.

"Yeah, I'm sure of it. Shhh, here you can have one," I whispered and handed her a small rock to hold. The line was moving forward, so I put the rocks back in the shape of a C.

The rations were a lot like what we had in Denver. We were told the meat would be wild game, and when they have successful hunts, we would get it twice in one month. The next three weeks dragged on with the typical chores while my parents worked. The only baseball I played was in the memories in my head. We had been here for almost a month. The summer was giving into the cold winter wind, and the threat of snow rolled across the coming September skies. I kept looking for Hayden or more signs that he was here, but all I had was a pile of rocks. It felt like the end of an inning with no one on base, two outs, and a full count. I haven't given up This game isn't over.

CHAPTER SIXTEEN

I often looked outside at the rugged mountains while working in the kitchen. Its snowy blanket was seeping down the mountain more each day. It would soon cover us, too. It was a hypnotizing view. I never tired of it, but a yelping sound broke the spell. I tried to see what it was out the window, but nothing. I left the last shirt in the washtub and went out the sliding door.

Outside was a small reddish-brown dog with wiry hair. It was limping, and I bent down to call it toward me. It shied away. I ran inside and got a small piece of meat from our fridge. By the time I got back outside, it was gone. I turned to go in, and I saw it peeking around the corner. I tore the meat into pieces, put one down, and backed away. She cautiously approached the meat and ate it greedily. I held out another piece. She got within a couple of feet of me and stopped. I again put it down, taking a few steps back. She limped forward, closer this time, and consumed the meat. She was thin, and hunger was winning out over fear. I had one more piece. If she wanted it, she had to come all the way to me to get it.

"Come here, girl," I said in a soothing tone. "I won't hurt you."

Inch by inch, she crept toward me, finally closing the gap between us. She ate the meat, and I carefully petted her coat while she licked the precious remnants off my hand. She was not fighting me now, and I looked her over a bit. I could tell she was young by her clean white teeth, but she was terribly thin. My dad loved to talk about the dog he had as a teen. They were great stories, and right now, I was grateful for all the information I got from them. Just then Mesh came out. I was worried that the dog would run away. She tucked her tail but wagged her little body in excitement. Cautiously, she made her way over to Meshka and licked her hand.

"Connor, she's so cute. Can we keep her?"

"Mesh, I don't know where she came from, and I doubt we'll get permission to keep her."

"She's hurt. We have to help her. She'll be scared. I hear the yippy dogs at night sometimes. They don't seem nice."

"No, coyotes aren't nice, that's for sure." My mind clicked into full scheming mode. Maybe the two of us could hide her for a little while, then who knows? "How much do you want to keep her?"

"Lots and lots!" she answered with enthusiasm.

"Okay. Let's put her in the garage, and I'll check out her paw."

"Is this a secret?" she asked.

"Yes, and I'll take the blame, so if Mom or Dad find out, say it was my fault."

"I'll keep the secret. Everyone else keeps secrets from me, and now I can keep one too."

Sometimes I forget that all this has happened to her too. I squeezed her tight, "I love you, Mesh."

She returned the hug and patted my back in a gesture of comfort. I scooped up the dog and went into the house. She had a cut on her paw, and I decided the best way to clean it out was to give her a bath. I emptied the last shirt from the rinse tub and sent it through the wringer.

I put her in the warm, soapy water, and she fought it, but she never turned on me. It made me wonder who had raised and trained her and whether they wanted her back. We washed her as well as we could, and I re-looked at her paw. It wasn't too bad. I grabbed a towel from the pile that hadn't been washed yet. She was a little uncooperative as I dabbed on the ointment we use for our cuts on her paw. I wrapped her foot in a thin dishcloth and tied it with twine, making sure it was appropriately snug. I carried her to the garage while Mesh got her a bowl of water. Clipping small pieces from every kind of food we had, I hoped it wouldn't be missed. Grabbing the extra blanket from my room, I set a box on its side, facing away from the kitchen door. She ate every crumb of the ration concoction. She licked Mesh's hand and soon settled down into a restful sleep.

The house was in perfect shape when my parents strolled in an hour later than usual. They looked beat. Good, I thought. They work tomorrow too, so they'll eat and go to bed early. That night, Mesh and I took turns going into the garage to keep the dog quiet. I was right; they went to bed early, and I said I'd tuck Mesh in and tell her a story. As soon as enough time had gone by, we snuck the dog into my room.

"We have to give her a name," I said quietly.

"Debbie," Mesh whispered.

"I've kind of been thinking about this all day. How about Liberty?"

"That's pretty."

"Yeah, well, it's not a word you can say around town. Liberty means freedom."

"Why do you keep saying words that are bad?"

"Freedom isn't a bad word. It just makes bad people nervous." I didn't expect her to understand.

Mesh rubbed the dog's ears and spoke baby talk to her. "Hey, how about Libby?" The dog was wagging her tail. "Look, she likes it too."

"Mesh, that's perfect!" I was about to suggest the same nickname, but she beamed with pride, and there was no reason to take it from her. "Libby, it is," I said, told her a quick story about our new dog, and got her into her bed. "Goodnight Mesh, good dreams."

"Night, Connor," and she rolled over onto her side, dragging her ringlets with her.

The dog slept with me, so she wouldn't bark or howl at night. I had no idea how this was going to turn out, but I needed Libby, Mesh needed

Libby, probably as much as Libby needed us. I woke up early and put Libby out back. She was happy to play outside, and her limp was already improving.

"Hey, look," my dad said. "Someone's dog is playing out in our yard."

"Huh?" I said.

"Huh," Mesh copied me, and I almost laughed out loud. Then she asked to see it, so my dad held her up to the window above the sink. It was a great distraction, and one that didn't have my dad running Libby off. Nice squeeze play, Mesh.

My parents left for work, and I sighed, relieved that we had gotten away with our deception one more day. I didn't feel as bad about deceiving them as I would have a couple of months ago because lately deception ran amuck in our house, and turnaround to get something for Mesh and me seemed fair. Mesh played with Libby all morning. I have missed Hayden so much, and I forgot Mesh lost her best friend too. But this morning with her new friend, she was as happy as I've ever seen her.

I may have made things worse. I fear we will have to give her up.

After lunch, we worked on teaching Libby her name and how to sit. She was a smart dog, and again I wondered where she came from. I figured if she had a home, she'd go there when we let her out, but she stuck to us like glue. Our schedule worked to keep our secret one more day, but tomorrow is my mom's day off. It seemed unlikely we would pull off the deception much longer.

"Mom, please don't be mad," I said when she caught me sneaking the dog out of my room.

Mesh came running around the corner, "It's all my fault, Mom. I found her, and Connor helped me take care of her. I miss Savannah so much, but now Libby makes me happy again. Please, please don't take her away."

I couldn't believe it, but my mom was melting like butter. It surprised me that Mesh took the blame when we had decided I would. She was cool as a cucumber, wrapping my mom around her finger. Mom helped us keep the secret for two more days.

Then, the unexpected happened.

I was awakened earlier than normal by my father shaking me. He saw the dog curled up beside me, and it stopped him in his tracks. I felt Libby's tail wag in anticipation of meeting a new friend.

But my dad was laser-focused when he said, "Don't speak. Get dressed, pack your tote, and bring it out to the front room and put that dog outside."

Confused, I sat up and saw him put my tote on the chair. I quickly got dressed, grabbed my hidden books, and stuffed them at the bottom of my tote. I prepared the castle the same way I did before and stuffed the rest of my belongings into the cloth bag. Libby waited eagerly to be let out for a pee break. Before I left my room, I looked over my shelf in the closet. Everything was gone except my meteorite. I snatched it quickly and stuck it in my coat pocket. I went to the kitchen, let Libby out, and immediately took the short walk to the front room.

A fully geared-up soldier was behind the partial wall between the kitchen and the front room. He didn't say a word, but he reached for the tote in my hand. I thought he was going to search it. Here I was again, after promising not to. I was risking everyone because I couldn't give up these items. I was afraid to give them up. I was afraid to leave them. I had to protect them as well as us, but I didn't know we were leaving—again. Why were we leaving again? I wondered what GD would do, what my dad would do, and what this soldier would do if he found the art book and the castle. Would my disobedience be taken out on my dad, us, and what about poor Libby? I swallowed hard and handed him my tote, and he just piled it into a cart with the three others that belonged to my family.

"Are we going somewhere else again?" I whispered to my mom. I was quiet because I could tell it was a secret moment, and I've had a lot of experience with secrets lately. People always have the same blank look with alert eyes trying to hide their fear. No one answered my seemingly logical question, but the soldier said in an electronic voice coming from his suit. "Please sign this contract," and he handed my dad a clipboard. My dad was busy reading the form. I knew this was my last chance to save Libby. I would take all the blame, and I didn't care what they did to me. I couldn't bear to lose another friend. I turned to the soldier.

"Please, sir, please let me take my dog. I need her, my sister needs her," Mesh came running over to me, hanging on to my coat while I cradled her with my arm. I was holding back my tears, but Mesh began full-on crying. My dad dropped the clipboard to his side and began approaching, but the soldier held up his hand, signaling it was okay. The soldier bent down to our level.

"Look, kid," his voice still using the speaker device, "I'll take her and see what I can do. Okay?"

I was stunned. He was... nice, at least I think he was. "Thank you, mister Neighwah, sir." I ran and got Libby, who was waiting at the backdoor and handed her to the soldier. My dad returned the clipboard to him, and he put it in the cart too. "I didn't feed her yet," I said, hoping I hadn't gone too far with my requests. He just nodded.

Before he left, he stopped and turned to me, "I'm not a Neighwah. I'm a Defender." He then grabbed the awkward two-wheeled cart, steering it expertly one-handed while carrying Libby tucked on his side in the other.

A Defender, I said to myself. The way he said it sounded... noble *and* defiant, like a knight. It sounded like being thought of as a Neighwah was insulting. At first, that sounded good, but then I thought about it a little more. Great, we're in the thick of two warring armies.

"What more could go wrong?" I said sarcastically under my breath.

My dad locked up the house and put the key back on the lip of the garage frame.

I stood there thinking about all the essential items we were again leaving. Maybe that's how moving is done in our territory, but what keeps the

Drangers from stealing all those items? They'd be gold on the black market. My dad started down the driveway, and I wondered if I was older and had the choice, would I follow him? I eyed my mom walking beside my dad, and Meshka looked up at me. My answer was quickly found, and it was yes. Yes, I would. These people, my family, were my whole world, and I would follow them into the darkest night. But I hope that's not what's happening now.

"I hope you know what you're doing, Dad," I mumbled and grabbed Meshka's hand.

CHAPTER SEVENTEEN

My dad walked down the road like a man on a mission. He was resolute and determined. I had no idea what he was resolved for or where he was determined to go, but I followed. I looked around at this beautiful location he was leaving without a second thought. He marched on, missing the dawn's twilight rays as they stretched across the tiny town, onto the bright new snow, and against dark, craggy rocks. It had successfully crawled down the mountain, spreading a thin white shimmer over the town. The workday would begin soon. It would begin the same and end the same and continue every day from then on. I wasn't sure which I preferred: the familiar or the unknown.

We walked on the snow-dusted road, leaving clear footprints in our wake. My dad saw them too, and I could tell they had his attention. But the morning sun would remove them very soon. Hopefully, our luck will hold out until then. We came to a large building that read *South Park High School*. My dad headed right for it, and I felt the need to remind him. "Dad, we can't go into schools."

"It's over an hour before school begins. We'll be gone by then."

"Where?"

He smiled and said, "Somewhere else." I smiled back. I smiled because it was ironic, and it was a private joke between us, not because it was funny. It was terrifying.

As we walked through the school, I noticed the damage it had endured. Windows were boarded up, the walls had bad language written on them, and many of the tall metal lockers that lined the halls had their doors twisted off their hinges. We passed a door, and above it, a small sign said *Science Lab*. I started reading the little signs, and I saw two more that interested me: *History* and *Social Studies*. I wonder if they learned the same things GD taught me. We went down the stairs and passed a huge room with another sign that said *Library*. It had shelf after shelf filled with books. I slowed down and looked through the window.

It held an astonishing number of shelves, and each one was brimming with books. What would it be like to have so many books to choose from? I had read all the books we had at our home in Denver at least twice. Granted, there were only seventeen, but this was like a pirate's hoard. I missed reading. I had my two secret books, but I had little time to spend with them. All we were given in Denver and Fairplay were the "boring packets of Corporate lies" or that's what my dad calls them. But looking at this room called Library, I could spend my whole life reading and never read the same book twice. Mesh pulled on my hand when I had allowed too much distance between her and her parents.

The damage was everywhere, probably in the library too. It began to anger me. I had never been in a school, but I assumed they would be nicely cared for. I couldn't imagine Dailys or Drangers being brave enough to damage schools, not like this. The Neighwah would shoot them on sight or put the whole neighborhood on alert until they found the culprit. Even if the occasional Dranger or Daily broke in, the damage could be repaired quickly enough.

I had heard Upper kids were brats, and they found their lives boring. In their boredom, they demolished things for fun. What I wouldn't give to feel bored. I never had that kind of freedom or time. They were ungrateful and destructive. How could they do this to their school? How could they not see what they had? What I wouldn't do to go to a real school, to be with other kids, read new books, talk about science and history, and play baseball. It would be a dream come true, and certainly better than working all day and aching all night. Didn't they realize how lucky they were?

I smiled then and had a GD memory. I remember him saying, "A person's point of view is hard to see when you're looking straight at them. You need to turn around and stand beside them to see what they see." I know how it is to be told I'm lucky by someone who didn't see my world through my eyes. Maybe these kids' gardens have weeds and secrets, and maybe they were fed so many lies, they are angry too. I hope Grandad's words never leave my head. They are the candles lighting my way through this dark world.

We came to a room at the back of the building. A piece of paper was stuck to the window in the door with a finger-to-lips picture meaning no talking was permitted. We went inside. At least a dozen other people were sitting there, obedient and quiet. I looked around, but no Hayden. My adrenalin was racing as I tried to imagine what was next on this crazy journey. The mood in that room was so intense, and I knew our very lives were on the line. It made me wonder what others had hidden in their minds and their luggage. The Defenders had taken our totes away in a vehicle, and I hoped they didn't find my stash of contraband. At least the people I was with would not get in trouble for my bad choices, but my dad would, and maybe Libby too.

A Defender motioned for us to go down the hall, and another one pointed outside to a large semi-trailer that was outfitted with rows and rows of bench seats. No one spoke, and I felt more like a prisoner than someone being protected. Maybe we *were* prisoners. Who knows what my grandad was involved in. It must have been pretty serious; he joined a rebellious group, stole valuable art from the Corporates, hid documents and weaponry, and who knows what else? My parents seem to have lost their minds. They left a secure home and good jobs that had them home before dinner time—twice. They ditched almost everything we owned and came to a smaller, more patrolled town where the winters could kill. And now, we were taking another trip to another somewhere else.

The numerous rows of bench seats were secured to the floor and faced the back. Several of the rows toward the front of the transport were already occupied with compliant captives. We dutifully climbed the ramp and into the windowless container. Filing down the aisles, we reached four available seats. The seatbelts lay lazily about the benches, and we buckled up. The door rumbled closed, and the finality of that sound made me shudder. I had no reason to trust this irrational plan that demanded submission without explanation.

When the door was secured, a Defender pressed a button on his shoulder and in a robotic voice told the passengers to buckle up. Some, like us before our van ride, weren't familiar with how to buckle them, but others offered help while remaining silent. I was anxious and wanted to get out of there. Yet, I remained, like everyone else, quiet, obedient, and trapped.

The four Defenders positioned themselves at the walls of the container and popped open small round slots. They stood facing forward with guns ready, while we all watched the monitors on each side wall. One Defender in the front turned toward the passengers and held his pointer finger against the front of his helmet to remind us to be quiet. All we had was a dull light from the ceiling and a fuzzy black-and-white view of the outside. A Defender motioned to another, and that Defender took a different position. I held Meshka's hand.

We were jolted in our seats when the transport jerked abruptly as it took off. We paused several times and rounded a few turns to get through the small town. Soon we began picking up speed and rocking around curves and aging roads. The excursion dragged on mile after mile. Occasionally we would stop, and the Defenders gestured for us to be quiet, then we would take off again. It seemed like quite a bit of time had gone by, and the younger children's patience was ending. At the signal of the person obviously in charge, one of the Defenders walked over to a box. I wondered what would happen to the babies breaking the rules, but the Defender simply opened the box and handed out water and meal bars to the passengers and bottles for the infants. He went back to his station, and the transport plowed on.

The meal bars were really tasty, and that surprised me because I expected them to taste like protein powder. Sometime later, the transport stopped, and everyone waited for it to start moving again, but it didn't. Wide eyes looked about, searching each other, hoping to see if anyone might be aware of what would happen next.

One at a time the Defenders pulled off their helmets, and it instantly transformed them back into humans. They were still full of weapons and intimidating, but then the woman in charge said, "Sorry for being so strict. Security is our most important weapon against discovery and attack."

Well, the good news was that she was being nice to us; the bad news was I had confirmation that we had dangerous enemies. A tall, young Defender addressed the rest of the group. "You may talk in a minute," he stated with such confidence and good English that he sounded like an Upper, which didn't help my weed garden. "Be careful as you exit down the ramp, and get in line to collect your bags from the transport parked across the parking lot. The attendant there will direct you to your registration line."

We released our belts and got into the shuffling line of people heading toward the ramp. The sun was bright and the air was crisp with the coming of autumn. The paved area was oddly painted in an odd camouflage pattern. Surrounding us loomed four huge buildings. There was a stream of people flowing from the baggage trailer which carried the luggage for the passengers on the transports now parked in between the four buildings. The crowd of bedraggled people, ladened with luggage, trudged over to a row of tables that stretched across the parking lot and then stood docilely in their assigned lines.

Everyone obediently walked from those lines to wait to be escorted into one of the buildings. It looked like ration day. Different lines for different people. Were some buildings for Dailys and others for Uppers? It wasn't looking like the "somewhere else" I had hoped for. While in the baggage line, I noticed two women pleading with a Defender. I could tell from their clothing they were Dailys. When one of them collapsed, I expected him to let her fall, but he caught her, and I heard him yell for a wheelchair. He seemed to be helping her.

I thought of Libby, and I hoped they were helping her too. Maybe she would be here, maybe Hayden too. That picked up my mood a bit. I grabbed my gear and Mesh's. No one asked me about my tote, which still had the weight of the castle inside. It gave me hope that I had gotten away with it. We were told to get in the line with the last three digits of our resident code on our luggage. I looked and printed on a tag looped through our tote handles read, NH4SW#090. A sign rose on a pole beside the tables, and I saw my dad and mom were headed to the one that read, 090-095. A soft mumble of voices hummed through the submissive crowd. Finally reaching the front of the line, I listened intently to the woman sitting behind the table.

"Welcome to the Hold," she said in a monotone voice. It was plain to see she had repeated these instructions many times. "Here are your identification bracelets. Please find the one with your name and put it on now before you leave this line." My dad passed my mom and me ours and secured his and Meshka's as the woman droned on. "They are used for meals, your lockers, checking out recreation items, and security. Do not remove them." She gathered some paperwork, put it in a folder, and handed it to my mother while Dad was busy with Meshka. "Take this to the line with the sign that says, *Alpha*."

There were several people in the *Alpha* line already. The Defender in charge of our line quickly verified our papers, and we were led away toward the building marked *Alpha*. We lined up again at the door, waiting our turn to be checked in. As we walked through the double doors, we entered a short hall with another set of doors at the end, guarded by another Defender. We stopped at the window when we crossed the entrance. Mom handed the Defender the file through the window. He opened it up and handed her back a map with our accommodation assignment circled.

"Use this map," he said, looking at my parents, "to locate your curtain and settle your belongings. Choose your locker side by holding your band up to the sensor. Once you use it, your locker is designated as yours. It will only open with your band. Your kids will do the same steps on their lockers, but your bands will open their lockers too. Feel free to use the restrooms and stop by the cafeteria for a snack sack. We follow military time here, which is explained in the binder located in your curtain. There will be a mandatory briefing for everyone at 1500 hours. Bring your binder." He looked straight at me. "Dinner is at 1630 hours. I figured you would want to know," he said and smiled at me. How could I not smile back? Not only were we assured of a dinner, but someone else was cooking!

This operation looked a lot like a strict camp, and again I questioned my parent's judgment. I was also pondering what he meant by "curtain". He said it several times like it was what our houses were called. We approached the second door and waited for the Defender to punch in her code. Once we passed through the entrance corridor, my curtain question was answered quickly with a disappointing visual.

CHAPTER EIGHTEEN

The first area we walked through was empty and enclosed by a high fence with solid panels on the bottom and chain-link on the top. Two tall poles sitting on opposite sides of the area sported big boards and a hoop at the top with a curtain of chains hanging around them. They looked like some kind of punishment device. With all the space between them, I feared we might have to witness punishments there.

Several gaps in the fence allowed traffic to pass in and out of the unused area. Through the fence, I could see an encampment of square-curtained rooms of various sizes. This is the sanctuary? I had much bigger expectations. In the first move, we lost our garden, space, and a lot of stuff. Now we have lost a lot more space, the rest of our stuff, a bathroom, and with no real walls, our privacy too.

My dad led us to Section 3, and we located our 090 curtain address. The sides were thick medium, grey canvas wrapped around poles at the corners. The door was two loose hanging sections of lighter canvas, ringed at the top for sliding apart. As we walked in, I could see both sides of the divided curtain home with the partial wall ending three feet in front of the entrance.

The ceiling was a thinner white material, and the lights from the building shone through, making it well-lit. One side had two fully made cots slid together, with the pillows against the back wall. Tiny nightstands sat like bookends on either side. A small desk and a locker were placed on the front wall next to the door. This was my parents' room.

The other, larger side was ours. Two neatly prepared cots sat with the pillow ends on the outside wall. Each had a nightstand, one in the back corner and one between the cots. Our locker sat toward the front end of the dividing wall, and a small round table with four chairs decorated the space by the entrance. On top of the table were the binder and a bag of toiletries.

Inside the bag were four hairbrushes, two razors, four toothbrushes, and a tube labeled toothpaste. No soap was issued, curious. Everything was new and unused. I'd never had a toothbrush or toothpaste before. We used our fingers and baking soda to clean our teeth. So, I went through a list of what we had given up: a kitchen, a private bathroom, actual walls, windows, and a way to do laundry. The only upside I could see was that everything was clean and new. I set my bag on the far cot and Meshka's on the one near the table.

"Dad," I said, trying to stay calm, "what..." I didn't finish before he interrupted me.

"I know! Trust me, my patience is wearing thin too. I have done everything they asked me without complaint, but this is NOT what I expected either." He sighed, "Let's wait until after the briefing to make any judgments. Okay?" He picked up the binder that said Alpha Hold from the table and started looking through it.

I sighed, nodded, and went over to the locker. It had two sides, and I held my band up to the black shiny square on the far one. It clicked and popped open. "Well, that's cool." Meshka came over and her band did the same thing. Just to check their theory, I closed Mesh's locker and tried to open it with mine. Nope. "Try mine, Mesh." That didn't work either. The open locker revealed a thin closet section for hanging things; shelves lined the other side, and a large drawer squatted at the bottom. I put my clothes and things away on the shelves, tucked my shoes at the bottom of the closet section, and hung up my coat.

As I put my baseball equipment on the shelf, I wondered if I would get to play catch anytime soon. I decided to be brave and leave my art supplies out. I figured I could say GD gave those to me. One more lie to tell and one more secret to keep from the people I loved. I should feel guilty, but I felt relieved that they hadn't found me out. I wondered if my life would ever get simpler. I wondered if I would ever be brave enough to follow the knight's creed.

I waited until Mesh walked over to our parents' side to hide my castle and museum book in the drawer. Unpacking didn't take long. We were down to almost nothing. It was then that I remembered our crates and GD's desk had still not been delivered. If they were, where would we even put them?

"Well," my mom said after a few minutes of settling the dwindling number of things we now owned, "how about we hit the bathroom and check this place out? I believe I heard something about a snack."

"Yeah," Mesh was jumping up and down, unbothered by any of it.

I had to admit, I was curious what a snack sack would contain, especially since the meal bar was so tasty. I tried to guess what GD would say at this moment. Probably something like, "What do you need right now that you don't have?" Well, I thought, Hayden, Libby, information, walls, and you. He would say those are wants, but they ache inside me like wants and feel like needles.

We went to check out the bathrooms first out of necessity. Three unisex restrooms were positioned among the curtain homes. Each one consisted of three connected shipping containers. On one end were five full-door toilet stalls, five sinks, and two small baths raised on a pedestal for bathing infants and small children. Through a connecting door were four shower stalls with adjacent changing areas. There was a laundry room on the other end, accessed through a door. Inside were three washers and two dryers. They were the push button kind, and a list of steps was posted on the wall by the washers, and another by the dryers.

Cooking and cleaning took up most of my days, so does that mean I'll have free time? Okay, I had to admit, it was looking better. When we entered the cafeteria space, I noticed at once the thing on the map called the lending shelf. There were all sorts of toys and books, lots of books. A young woman sitting at the bench table called out to them.

"Hey, come get your snack. You're going to love it." She was kind of excited to give them to us.

"Are those things on the lending shelf for Dailys too?"

She walked towards us. "What's your name?"

"Connor," I stood frozen. When they ask your name, you know you're in trouble.

"Well, Connor, you are not a Daily anymore. And you are welcome to everything on that shelf."

Talk about a changeup. I'm not sure how she could make me stop being a Daily, but she was the happiest person I had ever met. I smiled at her and took the sack she handed me. Mesh and I sat at one of the tables and opened the little bags. Inside was a small, flat biscuit, and next to it was an apple, a real apple, not freeze-dried.

"Holy cow." I bit into the little bread thing, and it was like nothing I had ever tasted. It was... I didn't have the words, but I had never had food that made me feel happy. Maybe that woman had eaten too many. It didn't take long to finish it, and I hoped we'd keep getting them.

"It's called a cookie," she said, seeing my face. "It's the chocolate chips that make them taste so good. I love welcome day," she said, still smiling.

"It's amazing," I said. Then I took a bite of the first and best tasting, fresh apple I had ever had. "Wow, apples are incredible when they're fresh."

"I know. Welcome to the Alpha Hold, the last stop before New Haven." With that, she got up and went into the kitchen area. What is New Haven?

There was a clock on top of the locker in our room. It was the circular type with numbers from one to twenty-three, and it had a digital display too. All Daily workers were issued a digital watch. I had seen them, but I wouldn't get one until I was thirteen. I usually woke up before the morning work horn, made lunch at the sound of the lunch horn, and started dinner at the end of the day shift horn.

Since telling time didn't apply to me yet, I didn't worry about learning it. But I guess I better start. We arrived a few minutes before the briefing. As we sat down, an announcement signaled the Welcome Briefing would start in five minutes. Well, if that keeps happening, I won't need to learn to tell time yet.

The trickle of people coming into the bench seats in the cafeteria stopped, and I looked around for Hayden, but again I was disappointed. The speaker headed for the front of the crowd. He was a man of average height, with a stocky build and big dark eyes. A wayward lock fell across his eyes, and he adjusted his deep brown hair behind his ear.

He approached a silver pole and lifted a cylinder out of its holder. He pushed something and then tapped on it sending thumping sounds throughout the area. The Neighwah used megaphones to address crowds. The small ones they held, and the big ones sat on their vehicles. This was the same thing, only a lot tinier.

"Good afternoon. My name is Haru Abar, and I will be walking you through this step of your journey to a new way of life. Up to this point, you have been kept in the dark about, well, everything. It was necessary because this idea of freedom is frightening to many Corporates. They would do anything to find out where we are and stop us from creating a free society. They know that if this idea gets out, it will develop a desire in every oppressed heart, and their rule will end." Subdued clapping came from the hesitant crowd.

"You have endured much to get here. You've been asked to trust in something with blind faith and subjected to severe, military protocols, but that's over now. Things will get better from this point on. First, no, this isn't your final destination; this is a holding area. We house you here for about a month until we know you don't have any contagions or issues that could threaten the 'sanctuary' we call New Haven. The belongings you packed up over a month ago have been sent ahead to New Haven. You won't need them until later because all your needs will be met while you are here. We will be meeting here every day to teach you and inform you about the group you have joined.

"The most important work we will be doing is learning how to trust and function as a free community. You come to us with a lifetime of being oppressed and betrayed. You all have terrible experiences and secrets from that world. These lessons will require you to let go of your defensiveness, your mistrust of others, and all the unhealthy coping mechanisms you have developed over the years." The whole crowd bristled at that statement, but he continued. "I like to say, we teach you to calm down that guard dog in your head. You will be taught to reach out to others and develop open, honest friendships. You will learn to respect, accept, and appreciate the uniqueness of others. This will not happen in the short time you are here, but we will give you the skills needed to live in a liberated community.

"Besides learning interaction skills, you will be educated in subjects that have been forbidden or portrayed untruthfully. Science, history, art, music, and others will be introduced and made available for you to explore on your own. You will also be given your job designation based on your achievements and skills tests. When you accept your job, your training for that occupation will begin."

He went on to explain the areas in the Hold and how to look up information in the binders. There was a whole section on schedules for everything. The part I liked best was that kids would spend this week learning to play and begin school studies. I found out the big open space was called the yard, and it was for playing. Haru told everyone to call him by his first name, even the kids. He told the parents that they would handle the family laundry because the machines were unfamiliar and required lessons. Wow, no laundry, no cooking, and little cleaning, it was too good to be true. My only chores involved learning and playing. I couldn't wait for the team sports activities, checking out a book, and dinner. If the cookie was any sign of the kind of food they serve here, I was in paradise.

They said dinner was early today because of the long and stressful day we had. We stood in a line to get our food dished onto trays. The signs said what each dish was called, and wondered if everyone here could read. Tonight's dinner was macaroni and cheese, a big piece of ham, fresh green beans, and another cookie for dessert. It was by far the best and biggest meal I had ever eaten. The helpings looked so big, but I ate every bit. I had never eaten so much, and my belly felt like it might burst.

I didn't even have to do the dishes. We just left our trays at the designated table. As full as I was, I headed over to the part of the shelf that held the books. I picked up a couple and decided on one about a kid on a river trip with his grandad. I thought about grabbing a ball, but no one else was out there, and I didn't want to be noticed by everyone. Besides, I told myself, I'm too full, and I want to start reading this new book. My family was leaving, so I used my band to check it out at the scanner in the middle of the shelf.

It was only 1700 hours, which is 5:00 in my old world. There were no windows in this building, so I get why they use military time. In the briefing, we were told we couldn't leave the building until transport day. As many cool things that this place has, I will miss the sun and the sky. GD says that people always find more to want; the key is to love what you have. I just have to focus on the good stuff. We got to our curtain and my mom said we should get cleaned up for bed.

"It's too early," I complained.

"We're not going to sleep yet. We're just getting ready before the bathroom is too crowded."

I set my book down and stuffed my clothing in my tote since we planned to take showers. I followed Mom and Mesh to the bathroom while Dad sat at the table, wanting to spend more time with the binder. There were about three other people there, and we didn't know any of them. One was a man, and the other two were teenage girls. Everyone was nervous about sharing the same space, but we washed our faces with soap from the pump thing and brushed our teeth with the little brushes.

The toothpaste left a surprisingly fresh feeling in my mouth. The girls thought so too, and they laughed about it. When the man left, we headed to the showers. I had never taken a shower before. We heated water on the stove and poured it into the tub. Mesh would take her bath first and then, while Mom got her dressed, I'd pour in another pan of hot water and take mine.

I walked past a shelf filled with bright white towels, so I grabbed one. Some of the doors said *with tub*, and I remembered Haru talking about the showers with shallow tubs at the bottom for small children. I wasn't a baby, so I was going to take a shower. I walked to the next door and opened it with my badge, and closed the door. The little room was divided into two areas. It had a changing area with a bench, and I put my towel on it. The shower was at the back. Though I had never taken a shower, I had been hosed off by Uppers once after they shoved me in the mud. I worried about standing in a stream of cold water, but I got ready and turned the handle as the instructions said. The water was warm, wonderfully warm, and clean.

The wall held three dispensers: soap, shampoo, and conditioner. I used the first two, but I didn't know what conditioner was, so I didn't try it. The showers were on a timer, so I hurried through washing and rinsing, and then I just stood there turning back and forth, enjoying the warm water. "Twenty seconds to automatic shutoff," a soft voice announced from the intercom above. I was done, so I just continued to soak in the rest of the time. I didn't mean to be wasteful, but it was so relaxing that my muscles just melted.

Back at our curtain, I lay down on my bed, getting ready to read. Mesh climbed into her bed and wanted a story.

"You know what conditioner is?" she asked.

"No, I saw it, but I didn't use it."

"Well, Mom put it on my hair, and I didn't have any tangles!"

"Oh, cool. My hair isn't as long as yours, but I can see how you would love that."

I told her a very quick story so I could get to reading my own. The bed was amazingly comfortable, with no lumps or sagging center. I snuggled into the clean, crisp sheets with no tears or patched-up holes and pulled the blanket around my shoulders. The weight of it was comforting. It was by far the best bed I had ever laid in. I started reading my book, but the big meal and warm shower floated me off to sleep before I finished the second page.

CHAPTER NINETEEN

I woke up to the announcement that the meeting would begin at 0900 hours. It was the best sleep I have had since this whole nightmare started. I was figuring out the military time thing. Just add twelve to the hours after noon. Like 2:00 in the afternoon would be 1400 hours. Now the clock said 0800 hours, so we had an hour to get there.

After another amazing breakfast, the older kids, thirteen to seventeen, stayed in the mess hall, which is the name of the cafeteria, to take placement tests to assess their educational needs. The little ones were led to a triangle area behind a partition next to the mess hall. They had brightly colored climbing cushions and interesting toys. The woman playing with them and the toys available seemed to have their attention, but they could see and access their parents if needed.

The twelve kids over five and under twelve were led to the yard where a dozen individual desks were pushed together. A young man told us to find our names and sit down. I found my name embedded under the glossy finish of the table and sat down. Mesh was next to me.

"Hi, my name is Theo, and I'm your teacher. Okay, look at your desktop." A group of six squares with different colors appeared to come from under the glossy finish of the desk. There were many oohs and ahhs at the electronic magic. He went on. "Touch the color you like best."

I touched red, and Mesh touched green. Another group of pictures came up, and we picked our favorites until we had six favorite items displayed on our screen. The computer display was fun, but this was baby stuff. I hoped it got more challenging soon.

"Stand up," he said. "Walk around the tables and touch each of the items that match your choices on each other's screens." I wondered if the kids would be too worried or scared to share information with strangers, but each kid obeyed, and we ended up back at our desks.

"As you can see, we have some things in common, but we are different too. I know you have been taught not to stand out and seem different, but today we start to change that." He went through the categories, and when he got to the foods, he said, "I see cookies are a hit with everyone." We all laughed because it was a safe thing to laugh about. It was as if he commanded we laugh, and we did.

"Okay, now this will be harder, but I want you to try. Everyone stand up. Now, find the people who like the same pet as you and stand with them, go." Slowly we meandered along, asking each other what their animal was, and we ended up in six groups. The cat lovers had four kids, the dogs had three, and two chose rabbits. Birds, butterflies, and lizards had one.

Those of us standing alone were noticeably uncomfortable, and I was anxious about what would happen to us. Maybe we answered wrong, and we would be used as an example to the rest. These weren't even the hard secrets. I could see that learning to trust and be open with strangers was going to be harder than I thought. Theo had our attention as we all waited for what came next.

"I can see some of you feel uncomfortable, but I hope to teach you to be proud of what makes you, you. It is the things that set us apart that make us unique, but we've been taught not to stand out and not be unique. Everyone has qualities and preferences that make them different.

It is these differences that keep a strong community inventing, improving, and thriving. It is liberty that sets these qualities free."

Mesh whispered, "Like our dog, Liberty." I smiled at her. A lot of what this teacher was saying was too hard for her to grasp, but she was listening and trying.

One blond-haired boy, named Teke, drummed up the courage to speak. "Was I supposed to choose the animal I want to take care of or the one I like to eat?" Everyone started laughing, even the teacher. It wasn't a laugh because it was safe; it was a laugh because it was funny. It broke the ice, and we got to more interesting games. There were some we played with other students and even some we played by ourselves.

He handed out headphones, and we listened to four songs. We were told to pick our favorite. I hadn't heard much music, and it all sounded good, but I finally chose a song with a lot of energy. Mesh picked a song with nice words, as she explained it.

When lunch came, we were starting to talk to each other without an assignment to force us. I met a girl named Alicia, and Teke, who made the rabbit joke. We talked on the way to the mess hall. Teke was here with his parents and older brother. Alicia was living with her dad. When we got to the mess hall, she went to her dad, Teke went to his family, and I went to mine. We did it because it was expected, but I wanted to talk to them some more. I wondered if we would ever get to eat with people who weren't our family, but I didn't want to be the one to ask.

Lunch was a sandwich called peanut butter and jelly, milk, and dried banana chips. Everything was tasty. When we came back, the tables were gone. Five big balls, Theo called beach balls, sat where the desks had been. Boxes were drawn on the floor, and we were told to stand in one. The game was to keep the balls in the air without leaving our square. Theo threw the balls up one after the other. That was super fun. That night, after another delicious meal, I lay in bed and read my book. It was exciting, and I wished I could boat down a river someday.

A couple of days later, we were in a triangle area behind a partition set up by Haru's office. It was our turn to take the assessment test now that we were trained to use the computers. The tests started easy and got harder if we got the correct answers. My test had articles to read, and then there were questions on what they were about. One was on a general named George Washington. He was called the "father of our nation" because he fought in the war to make the United States its own country and was the first president.

Another one was on flags and what they represent. The two flags discussed were the Colorado state flag and the United States flag. All the pictures and colors mean something, and then they described how the banner should be cared for and displayed with respect. I recognized the United States one as the cloth inside GD's shelf, and I remembered folding it with my dad.

The last one was on meteorites. It examined how they came to be, and how they followed an orbit until something knocked them out into space. I wonder what knocked the meteorites that hit us out of their orbit. Most of the kids hated those parts of the tests because they couldn't read well, but I loved them.

After lunch, we got to act out a skit about how people can think differently and still get along. It's not about being friends with everyone. It's about being respectful and learning about each other that builds a community. The story was about six people stuck on an island together, waiting to be rescued. Two of the characters became good friends right away. The other characters struggled to understand each other.

One night they started sharing their stories when they noticed one of them was missing when the fire died down. He was the one who was the best at building fires, and they realized he was a great asset to the group. They all pitched in to find him. After that, all the characters sat at the fire and discussed the gifts they each brought to their group. Each member was valuable to the group as a whole, and they decided to work through their personality differences to become a team and watch out for each other. It was a nice story. I wondered if it would work that way. I hoped so.

When we finished discussing it, I heard the older teenage kids playing in the yard. Theo gave us permission to get up and see. They were bouncing orange balls and trying to throw them through the hoops with chains. I was wrong about it being for some kind of punishment. Theo said it was a game called basketball. It didn't seem difficult, but it must be harder than it looks because they missed a lot. I hoped I would get to try it.

We had arrived on a Monday, and it had been a week of fun without any chores. Today was Sunday. Most of it was free time, but some of it was used for health checkups. Every morning we had a quick scan for temperature and oxygen levels at breakfast, but these appointments were more detailed. In the binder, it described them. The physical check was in two sessions, then there was dental and mental.

They used all sorts of machines to figure out if we were healthy. Today, our group was assigned to go to the mental health station. We each got to talk with Haru. After that, the rest of the day was ours, so Mesh and I went to the yard.

While Mesh and I waited our turn to check out the scooters, I read her a story with pictures from the lending shelf. I had just finished when it was our turn. They were playing music, making it fun to scooter to the beat. There was a path marked on the yard. It was cool how they could mark it and clear it off easily, but it didn't come off when we walked, ran, or rode over it. We had a great time riding the scooters. When I got back to the curtain, I took out my paper and art supplies and practiced drawing. I was getting good at drawing lizards, so I decided to add wings.

"Wow, Connor! That's really good. Who taught you about drawing and dragons? Never mind, I bet it was my dad." My mom smiled. She didn't worry about the supplies, and she filled in the lie for me. We had only been here a week, and this place was changing us. Maybe it was because we felt safe, fed, and... free.

That night we all brought our folding chairs and blankets to the mess hall. All the bench tables were folded up and pushed to the edge. A big screen hung down from the ceiling. For the first time in my life, I watched a movie. It was called a cartoon because everything was shown in drawings, but they moved and spoke, and sang songs. Knowing what I know about the difficulty of drawing, I was thoroughly impressed. It was colorful, loud, and incredible. Next week they will show two movies. One will be a cartoon, and the other will have real people in it.

In week two, my parents found out what their jobs in New Haven would be. My mom was going to work at the Town Hall as a secretary for the government. My dad was going to be a manager at the maintenance building. They were excited about their new careers. They were given computer tablets with information on their new positions and lessons to prepare them. They engaged with others in similar occupations to discuss topics and answer questions. At night, my parents dove into their lessons with genuine excitement.

I was excited about the announcement of games such as badminton, basketball, beach ball volley, bingo, and Frisbee games scheduled to be played in the yard. They were for adults, but we could listen to the rules and watch them play, which was fun. Then, we could play those games during the day while they worked in the mess hall. I even taught my class to play a baseball game I made up using beach balls.

Board games and cards could be played during the day in between meals at the mess hall or checked out to play at your curtain. It amazed me how quickly I was getting used to this life without threatening situations and weary workdays. It had all been replaced with good meals and learning, and instead of down-turned heads, people looked up and smiled at each other. It was like hitting the winning home run every day or pitching a perfect game.

It seemed too good to be true. I still had questions. What happened to Hayden and Libby? Where were our crates with our stuff? And then there was that pesky art shelf thing. These people knew about it because they took it. Did they notice the dragon box was open, and the book was missing? Were we in trouble? Was I?

My Grandad stole those things, and he was a Daily. My dad and I both knew about it and didn't report it. What will they do about that? They keep telling us we aren't Dailys anymore, but I don't know how that works inside people's heads. I didn't want to seem unappreciative. I didn't want this dream to end. So, I didn't push my luck by talking about it.

CHAPTER TWENTY

During week three, Theo paired us up with kids close to our level of education according to the test we took. I found out that some of the games we played were part of the test. The lessons were getting a little harder, but we still took time for fun activities. This week the adults were busy practicing actual tasks that they would do at New Haven. There were all kinds of contraptions set up in the mess hall.

Most mornings, Haru gathered us all together for a short meeting before we went to our assigned areas for the day's lessons. He often talked about the "emotional journey from oppression to self-determination," but today he talked about our physical bodies. Haru said many of us had mild to severe cases of malnutrition, and we should be noticing the positive effects of regular, healthy, and ample meals. It's true. I've noticed changes in myself. My clothes fit a little tighter, and before we came to the Hold, I learned to ignore my belly telling me I was hungry.

I mean, I knew I needed food, but I didn't crave it. But now I look forward to mealtime, and my stomach growls incessantly. I sleep better than I ever have. When I get up in the morning, I feel full of energy and gumption, as GD would say. And I can think so clearly that I read and do math faster with more understanding.

One cool thing that happened this week was Haru said there would be a wedding celebration. I had seen a wedding picture of my grandad and my grandma. They were dressed very fancy, and there was a big party with food and a cake. Dailys got married at the registration building, and that was it. No one had the same days off, so we couldn't have parties. But people who knew them often gave them things for their house from their might-need-it boxes. I didn't know what the Hold would do for a wedding, but so far, they did things way fancier than I was used to, so I was excited to see it. But the most exciting news was the mini farm.

We learned that chickens and rabbits were being kept in another section of the building. The animals were also in quarantine before going to New Haven. The tiny livestock would be used in conjunction with a new technique that took an ounce of meat and duplicated it ten times, so a few animals would go a long way to supply more protein to the New Haven diet. The people chosen to work in the farm and ranch sections suited up to go work with the animals and their mentor. The residents, that's us, bombarded them with questions when they returned.

I waited for the right time to ask about Libby. It was just before dinner and people were in their curtains and too busy to notice me. I had to be brave. I had to know. I had left our curtain saying I had to use the bathroom when I saw a Defender alone and heading to the hospital door. I wasn't sure where the animals were, so I quickly walked over to her. I guessed she was a woman Defender because she was short. All the guy Defenders that I had seen here were taller. She was dressed in full gear, with her helmet on and face guard down. It made me wonder if there was something dangerous in the hospital. But I just wanted to ask her a question. She was holding up her badge to the scanner and was poised to punch in her code.

"Miss Defender, ma'am, I was wondering if my dog Libby was in the Animal Hold." I was starting to shake, afraid I would get in trouble or get my parents in trouble. What if they lost their jobs because of me? But I continued, "They took her when we came here and said they would try to get her back to me. If it's not any trouble..."

Before I could finish, she looked around the building and said, "Hey, let's go see." She shoved me through the door. She must have been in a terrible hurry because she pushed me down a long hallway. She opened a door and told me to wait for her, and that she would bring Libby to me. That's when she closed the door, and I heard her lock it. It was pitch black in there, but I felt around and finally found a light.

There were tons of boxes piled on shelves full of all kinds of supplies. I could tell it wasn't a place where I should be, waiting for a simple answer. I sat there for what seemed like a long time, and the worry weeds came back in full force. I was in danger. Maybe this place was all a lie, and when you ask questions, they get rid of you. Maybe they knew what I had done and all about the weapons and art stuff, and now I was in trouble.

"Grandad," I said quietly to myself, "please help me. I've tried to be brave. I'm sorry I opened the dragon box. I don't know what to believe anymore. Why did you steal that art? Why did you have those boxes with ammo? Were there guns in the other ones too? And why did you leave me to deal with all of this alone? If you were still here, I wouldn't be worried about the shelf. I can't even think of a baseball situation that is this bad. You would have found a way to explain things to me, but now I'm alone again. I've lost you, I've lost Hayden, I've lost Libby, and now... now."

I heard someone at the door. Maybe she was bringing Libby. I turned out the light like she left me, so she wouldn't get mad. The door opened, and it was a different Defender with no helmet on. I was so scared, I scurried to a corner. I knew he could hear me because I was trembling and gulping back shaky breaths.

"Hey, Connor. Come out bud. Everything is going to be okay." He sounded sincere, but I lost it when he came back to where I was hiding, and then I blacked out.

When I woke up, another Defender was carrying me to the hospital. "Don't kill me. I'm sorry. I didn't know," I pleaded.

He laid me on a hospital bed, saying, "Relax, kid, you're going to be okay."

"Connor," a woman in a white coat looked at me with eyes like Maylee and little Dace. I have lost so many people in a short time. I thought of me losing Grandad, Hayden losing his mom, and Dace and Alicia losing their fathers; hospitals were horrible, painful places where people die. I turned onto my side, and although I was breathing in fast pants, I felt like no air was getting to my lungs. I tried not to make any sound, but the tears rolled in a steady stream down my face. "Connor, I'm Doctor Maya. I am so proud of how brave you were. Can you turn and look at me?" I turned, hoping this wasn't another trick. "I'm going to put this mask on you. It will give you more air and help you catch your breath." I didn't want it, but I was too scared to say no.

"I need to know," Dr. Maya said, "did the Defender hurt you? Are you in any pain?" I shook my head no. The air was working, maybe she was helping me. A woman Defender came into the room, and I flinched. Maybe she was the one. I remembered the cornered mouse. I imagined I was that mouse, seeing all these people looking down at me, deciding my fate. The woman Defender walked up to stand by my bed.

"Hi, Connor. I'm Hannah. I'm sorry a Defender treated you so badly. That's not how we are trained to treat people, especially children. This is not your fault, and you are not in any trouble. In fact, you're kind of a hero. You're safe. We caught her, and she's in custody."

"How?" I said in an unsteady, muffled voice.

"You caused her to take too much time to hide you, so she didn't get to steal the information she wanted. She went to a lot of trouble not to hurt you. Can I ask you some questions? Nothing you tell me can get you into trouble. I promise." I thought about some of the secrets I knew, and I wondered if she could make such a promise. But I nodded. "Why did you go over to her? What did you say?"

I took a big breath. I didn't know what lie would work, so I decided to tell the truth. Pulling the mask off my face, I answered. "I asked her about

Libby." I could feel the tears pushing at the back of my eyes, but I held them back.

"Who is Libby?"

"My dog," I explained finding her, and what happened on leaving day. She was smiling.

"That's a great story. I love that. Then what did she do?"

"She said, let's go find her. She pushed me through the door and made me walk quickly down the hallway. She told me to wait for her in that room. Then she closed the door, and it was dark, so," the tears started coming and my breath got shaky again, "I found the light switch, and then when I heard someone at the door, I turned it back off because I thought I'd get in trouble, so I hid." The crying took over. "I'm sorry. I didn't want to cause trouble, I just..." I tried to be brave, but I couldn't make it happen. My words came in deep sobs, and I tucked my knees up to my chest and buried my head between them.

Hannah secured the mask back on my face and put her arms around me. "I think you should get Haru and tell his parents he's safe. I need to find Gray."

After I calmed down, Dr. Maya gave me some juice and put a rolling ball up to my chest. I could see my lungs and my heart on the screen. She put the mask back on my face and told me to try to make my heartbeat slower by taking slow, easy breaths. She had a soft voice, and I started to feel calmer. My heartbeat took on a steady pace, and my lungs went in and out in a regular pattern.

By the time Haru came in, I had myself settled down. "Hi, Connor. Do you remember me?"

"Yeah, you're the guy who helps us change our feelings."

He laughed, "That is giving me more credit than I deserve. But what I can do is help you understand your feelings, and that can help you decide what to do next. I'm sorry about what happened to you. We worked so hard to make you let down your guard, and then you got ambushed. You have every right to feel betrayed, but I hope you will give this place a second chance. I'm going to have you go back to your mom and dad right now. They are very worried about you, but we are going to talk more later, okay?"

"Okay. I'm not in trouble, right? Everyone said that I wasn't."

"The Defender who took you is in trouble, but you are not. Not in any way at all."

The Defender who had carried me to the hospital came through the door. "Are you ready to see your family, kid? They are anxious to see you." I got up and followed him into the yard. My parents ran over to us and hugged and scolded me at the same time, but I didn't care. I was just glad to be back in their arms.

The next day the wedding came and went. Everyone was excited by the flowers made from napkins and the ring someone had donated. The groom wore black pants and a white button-up shirt loaned to him by a Defender. Several men stood next to him, and Haru stood in front. The bride was in a white dress, which made a striking contrast with her rich, dark skin. A flowy belt was tied in the back and floated behind her. Her hair was full of little braids, and they spilled all down her back and the sides of her face. She was the prettiest woman I had ever seen.

The kitchen staff served sparkling juice and sweet pastries, usually saved for Sunday breakfasts. There was music on the speaker, and everyone danced. The bride threw her bouquet away, and another woman caught it, but quickly gave it to someone else. I'm not sure what that was about, but I don't care either. I sat through the whole celebration and never moved. I felt damaged and nothing seemed the same anymore. I still didn't know about Hayden, his family, or Libby, or when the shelf thing would come crashing down on me. Tick, tock, it was just a waiting game now, and the weeds were so tall, I was hiding in them.

CHAPTER TWENTY-ONE

The morning after the wedding, I had my appointment with Haru. I told him about my grandad, my family, moving, and stuff like that. I told him about Hayden and Libby. And he said he would look into both of those things. He even promised. I want to believe him, and I'm going to try because it's my only hope.

After we had talked for a couple of minutes, he asked what I was most afraid of. I froze, and he saw it. He didn't even know me, and he could read my signals.

"Let me try and guess," he said. "You fear you won't find your friend, and that maybe something bad happened to him and his family." I just sat there. Anyone could guess that. "You worry the same about your dog. You fear losing your grandad's home is like losing part of him again, and you won't get it back. You fear every step of this journey has been one loss after another, and nothing is going to change. Am I doing okay so far?"

"Well, yeah, but I kind of already told you those things, well, mostly." I was feeling anxious and defensive, and I wondered if he knew.

"Fair enough," he said and smiled. "You're very smart, you know that, right?"

I smiled and shrugged my shoulders. I didn't think he knew I was a Highmind, and I wasn't going to tell him.

"So, I have a couple more guesses. You are worried this place isn't what it seems. You're worried we know your secrets, and it is going to end badly for you and your family." He had me there, but I still wasn't going to confess. Everyone has secrets. Maybe this was how they got people to tell them things, and then they'd deliver the punishment.

"I don't mean to be ungrateful for everything, but more bad things happen to Dailys than good things. I know I'm not supposed to think of myself as a Daily anymore, but I do."

"It's going to take a long time for those feelings to go away. You are not alone in that fear. Every single person here, if they are honest, has the same worry.

"Is everyone here a Daily?"

"No, some were Uppers, some were Neighwah and Drangers, and we even have a former Corporate. They gave up those titles and beliefs. But they have worries too. They worry you won't accept or trust them, and you will judge them."

"Huh, well, I think they may be right. It will be hard to trust non-Dailys. They were cruel and selfish. I saw what their kids did to their school and that's messed up." I was shocked people like soldiers and Uppers were involved. It did nothing to gain my trust.

"We are all messed up right now. We must learn to change and let others change too. We all deserve a new start. We all have secrets, and we've all done things to survive that we feel bad about, but we have to let those things go. Surviving in a hard world makes criminals of us all. We need to forgive ourselves and others for staying alive and let go of our worries."

"GD called them worry weeds. He said you had to keep cutting them back, or they will kill your garden."

"I like that, an excellent metaphor. I like that you gave him a nickname. It says you two had a special connection. Tell me more about him."

I talked for a while about GD. I talked about baseball and meteorites and the history I shouldn't know. He assured me I would get a lot more science and history at the New Haven school. It felt good to think about going to school and to have Haru say how much he wished he had known my grandad. Haru reminds me of him a little. He says thoughtful things that hang with me like my grandad's GDisms. He told me that even though my grandad was gone, his wisdom was my walking stick and lantern. Wisdom carries us through life and steadies us when the road gets rough, and it shines our way through the darkness.

I thought about what he said about wisdom. GD used to say wisdom is the light that pulls truth from the darkness. I couldn't wait to get time alone with the castle to try some things. I wasn't ready to spill my secrets, but I liked Haru and couldn't wait for tomorrow's visit.

It was the Monday of our last week in the Hold, and for most of this week, the kids would be joining their parents for morning activities in the mess hall. Haru signaled for everyone's attention.

"This is our last Monday in the Hold, and I know I'm not the only one who has noticed our remarkable transformation. We began our journey as isolated individuals and families, fighting a treacherous world alone. But today, we are a caring community willing to reach out to each other. I have witnessed genuine concern for fellow members and watched close friendships develop. Heck, we even had a wedding! I am so proud of all of you. You will soon join a much bigger community, and I know you will continue to practice what you have learned.

"Week four is all about continuing your notebook lessons and learning about New Haven. The first thing you'll be happy to learn is that the people here are your neighbors in New Haven. Your resident code is your new address. The 'NH' is for New Haven, but you probably guessed that. The next number is your floor plan designation, which means the size of your house. The SW denotes you will be in the southwestern section of the town. The last number after the hashtag is your street number. So, go, walk, talk, and compare."

I followed my parents as they met the people who had addresses next to ours. On one side there was a woman with the two giggly teenage girls from the bathroom. The older one was named Melody, but she liked to be called Mel, and the other was Amanda, but liked Mandy. They didn't say, but it was clear their father was gone from their lives. Like so many others, he was lost to a cruel world.

On the other side of us are two single women. It seems I'm surrounded by them. They were sisters named Jilly and Ari. I suddenly realized they were the two women talking with the Defender when the one named Jilly collapsed. She looked fine now, though. Jilly was sweet to Mesh, but I wanted to find out where Alicia and Teke lived, so I left the group.

"Hey, Teke," I said, and he turned around. "What's your number?"

"096. What's yours?"

"090. Have you seen Alicia? What's her number?"

Just then, Haru called everyone back to their tables.

"She's 101," he yelled over the shuffling feet and last-minute conversations. So, Teke was four houses down and Alicia was nine. I wondered how far away that was in this new town, this New Haven.

Next, we were separated into groups with similar family sizes and floor plans. He told everyone to find the floor plan he had just sent to each tablet. My parents connected to their notebooks, and I about dropped. These were the houses my grandad designed! We'll be living in Grandad's house after all. My mom hugged me, seeing me so excited for the first time in days. "You get your own room again, and no more having to make meals." I let her think that was it, but I wished I could share what I knew with her.

I looked over at my dad, hoping to get a secret nod about the housing layouts, but he just smiled back like he didn't even remember the designs. I thought back, remembering he didn't even look at them. He just stuffed them back into the shelf compartment as quickly as he could.

Haru, again, signaled for our attention. "As you can see, you have no kitchen," Haru continued. "You will still have community dining, but there will be opportunities to eat some meals at your house or have a picnic at one of the parks. We'll discuss that later. Next, open the furnishing link I just sent you. It displays the furniture your house is provided. Due to the organization of moving so many people into the site, your furniture is already installed in your home. But you may rearrange it when you arrive."

A hand went up in the crowd. "How many people are going to be there?"

"That is not a number I can tell you today, but there will be more. Okay, of the two neighbors closest to your street number, one will share a small yard with you. The town map is classified until we arrive, so I can't tell you which it will be."

"We get yards?" an excited shout rang out.

Haru called us together one more time. "I'm sure you have a ton of questions. Send them to me from your notebook, and tomorrow, I will answer the ones I can. Because it seems pointless to say work on your studies, no lesson work is due until Wednesday, but it's back to a normal work schedule tomorrow. See you then."

CHAPTER TWENTY-TWO

I sat at the lunch table on my own. I was trying to untangle the wisdom clue of the castle. My family had finished eating lunch and went back to the curtain to finish their lessons, so I couldn't pull my castle out. I was deep in thought when the head Defender, Gray Dakota, came over and sat with me. He wanted to make sure I knew the Defenders were here to protect me, and he apologized that one of his soldiers mistreated me.

I told him it wasn't his fault. Somehow the conversation turned to baseball. He knew of the game, but he never learned it. We sat for a while as I explained it. He had to go, but he promised to play catch someday. I noticed a small thin flashlight attached to his belt.

"Hey, Officer Gray," I said, calling him by his first name as he said I could, "may I borrow your light? It's for a science thing. I don't have to have it, but I wanted to try some experiments." He considered me for a moment and pulled the cylindrical item from its holster. As he reached for it, his shirt sleeve tightened around his muscular arms. He was extremely strong, and I bet he would be fierce in a battle.

"I can't see the harm in you using it. I do want it back, though."

"I'll give it back to you after dinner tonight." He nodded and smiled. He looks powerful and a little scary, but mostly he's awesome.

I went to my appointment with Haru right after lunch. We talked about the night our garage burned down and my dad getting beat up. He even gave me a book from the lending shelf called *The Boy Who Saved Baseball,* by John Ritter. It had a guy in a baseball uniform sitting on a bench with a kid. I couldn't wait to read it. But the thing that shocked me to my core was what he said at the end of our meeting.

"You know, Connor, your grandad did a great service to the world."

"How is that?" I said, putting my guard up around my secrets.

"You know you don't have to carry your secrets anymore. We asked your Grandad to design all the houses and many of the other buildings in New Haven. He also helped us hide those pieces of very precious art. We check everyone's bags, and we saw the art book and knew it belonged to the confiscated exhibit. We didn't want to scare you, and there didn't seem to be any harm in letting you look through it, so we didn't take it.

"Before the Corporates took over completely, we hid art wherever we could. We had to. They would have selfishly kept it all for themselves and used the pieces to gain more power. Some have even destroyed art as a way to control artists. But those pieces of art belong to the people, and they have no right to take them. They don't care about art. Everything is about control to them.

"But we will display it where it can be enjoyed by everyone in New Haven, and someday it will be given back to the world. In the meantime, it will be cared for properly in the New Haven Museum. I just thought you should know, but I ask you not to say anything until we get there, and we were hoping you could give us back the book of the art."

"I was sure my eyes were wide open with shock. All I could say was, "We have a museum at New Haven?"

"Yeah," he laughed. "It's nice too. Do you still have it?"

"Yeah. Do you mean all the pictures in that book are the pieces kept in my closet? I'm sorry I kept the book. I just really wanted to learn about art." I had gone through the book often, but I gravitated toward Vadina, the dragon. I should have spent more time reading about the other ones.

"I understand. No harm done. But please get it back to me. In this world, you can never tell what will happen next, and I don't want you to have it in your possession when we travel to New Haven. You took a big risk having it with you the first time, but none of that is your responsibility now. You can let us deal with those worry weeds from now on."

"So, we have a place where I can go see art when I want to?"

"We most certainly do," and he laughed at my reaction.

"Will there ever be science and history things like baseball history?"

"Well, I'm not going to give away all the surprises. You can go now. I think your appointments are done for now. We'll meet up after move-in, okay with you?"

"Okay, but we're still friends though, right?"

"Absolutely, we are."

"Thanks for the book," and I held up the novel he loaned me. "I'm meeting Officer Gray after dinner. Can I give it to him?" Haru nodded. "I'll return this one when I'm done. Wait, is there a library there?"

He just shrugged his shoulders and gave an expression like it was a secret. I laughed.

I was walking on air coming out of his office. On my way back to my curtain, I saw Jilly sitting on her chair in front of hers. She was working on her tablet, and I didn't want to interrupt her lessons, but as I walked by, she called me over.

"So, Connor, how are you? I guess we're neighbors now. I've thought about you often, and I'm sorry about what happened to you."

"I'm fine," I said rather quickly while stuffing my hands in my pockets.

"Uh-huh, well I know I wasn't fine when I first got here. I was attacked too."

"I saw you faint when we were standing in line. You got attacked?"

"Yeah, Ari and I were walking to the transport in Breckenridge. When this guy jumped out of a doorway and grabbed Ari by the arm, so I pulled out my little knife, jumped on his back, and stuck him."

"Whoa!" I responded. I thought of what Haru said about everyone doing bad things to survive.

"I know, right? But then he turned and punched me in the stomach hard. He had a ring filled with poison. I was in the hospital for most of the first week, and Ari got a broken arm. I don't know about you, but I was terrified. And sometimes, I wake up and I'm back being jumped over and over. But I'm glad you're fine. A big, strong kid like you can probably take care of himself."

"I wasn't brave at all," I said, and I dropped into the empty chair next to her. "I cried like a punk baby, and she didn't even hurt me."

"Of course, she did. I think being terrorized is worse than physical pain. It stays with you longer and takes your world. I can't stop worrying about it happening again."

I told her of my grandad's saying about worry weeds, and she nodded her head. "Isn't that the truth?"

"You know," I said, "you should talk to Haru. He's helped me not be so afraid."

"That's good advice, Connor."

Out of the corner of my eye, I saw Officer Gray walking toward us. "Is he your boyfriend? I see you two together a lot."

"Gray?" she saw him approaching, and she shrugged her shoulders. "I'm not sure what we are, but he definitely has put some weeds in my garden." We laughed, and she said, "Hey, we're neighbors. Come talk with me anytime."

"Thanks," I smiled and left her to go to my curtain. On my way, I thought of my mom having to let the Defenders see her ring. Now I knew why. It seems like a lot of the secrets are coming out, but not all. When I got to our curtain, I saw that my family was still there, so the castle would have to wait.

Before dinner, a volleyball game was scheduled between the adults. My dad went to play, and my mom and Mesh went to watch. I asked to stay behind to finish my lessons. I had already finished, but I needed to get to the castle before I had to give Gray his light back.

The first thing I did was turn the top of the tower again. There had to be something to direct me to the next clue. As I turned it, I heard a little shuffle sound. I did it again and used the light. Nothing moved, so again I put it back. Noticing the round hole on the edge at the top of the tower, I shined the light into it. I could see a light coming through a window in the back, and it showed on the curtain dividing our rooms. Ah ha. Keeping the light in place, I turned the tower top to the north, and the window showed an image on the curtain. It was a T-shaped image, like the one sticking up in the center of the tower. I pushed it gently, and it snapped down.

As it did, a carved bush flipped down, and a knight popped up in front of the tower. Cool! So being gracious was the next step. It seemed obvious that the G was referring to the knight on guard. Gracious, how would a guard be gracious? I imagined a royal court with people of the time. He might help someone, he might fight an enemy, he would, of course! He would bow before the king! I pushed on his back, and he folded forward, revealing a small tool sticking out of his back.

I heard my family coming, and I put my fortress back in my locker.

CHAPTER TWENTY-THREE

Day two of week four was craft day. "In your new home, Haru explained, the wall colors and window shades are all in neutral colors. Months ago, on your packing day, your family unit was told to choose a color scheme from four combinations. They included: cool grays and whites, mocha tans and off-whites, sage greens and off-whites, or smoky blues and whites. The interior of your house was painted in those shades. The exterior of your house was painted to go with the houses on your block.

"Today, you will craft decorative items to make your house into your home. The choices include pillows, rag rugs, tie-up blankets, placemats, flower arrangements, and wall décor. Each resident is allowed two items. You are also allowed to pick out three new outfits to fit your new lifestyle.

"Although I hope you have fun creating your treasures, don't neglect your studies. The assignments are short this week, but they're still due by the end of each day." He signaled the end of the session, and people went shopping.

There were plenty of craft supplies, all arranged in kits. I decided to make a rug to put in front of my bed and a blanket for cold nights. My mom helped Mesh make the same for her room, and she chose a blanket, flowers, a rug for the bathroom, and a welcome sign for the front door. Video directions were linked by the barcode found on the kits to notebooks. Only adults had notebooks, so they set up the student desks for us kids.

There were numerous racks of clothing, and they were arranged by size. I didn't even know what size I was. I don't remember ever shopping for clothes because we got hand-me-downs and adjusted them to fit. But the lady helping us said I was a size ten, and she helped me find the types of clothes I wanted. I remembered seeing the nice clothes the Upper kids wore, so I described them to her. She told me what they were called, so I could find them.

I picked out a pair of blue jeans, a pair of tan cargo pants, and some dark grey sweatpants to play sports in. I also chose a red Henley T-shirt and a light blue button-up shirt. There was a rack of long and short-sleeved tops showing people playing sports, and I chose a t-shirt with a guy throwing a baseball. We were also issued a clear sealed bag with underwear, socks, three white t-shirts, and special clothing to wear at night called pajamas. It doubled the number of clothes I brought to the Hold. I looked at my old clothes, and they appeared even more ragged after seeing my new ones. But I wasn't going to get rid of them yet because my new clothes felt stiff, and my old ones were a lot softer.

We were called to an emergency meeting on the third day of week four. A threat of exposure from radioactive clouds was heading our way. I guess that old man was right about the nukes. I wondered what had happened to him. It was decided to put the studies and projects on hold and move up the departure day. The original plan was that the residents would leave, and the packing of the facility would be completed by some of the Defenders. Since we had to hurry, everyone was employed to begin packing up the place.

The weeds came back with a vengeance. What do I do with the castle? I was so close to finishing it. It belonged to my grandad, and I know he meant it for me. I was the only one who could open it. It was just a puzzle.

The problem was, it was in a vulnerable state with the little knight bent over and the tool sticking up. It was so tiny, and if it fell out, the prize at the end would be lost. I delicately pushed on the knight, and he clicked back into his upright state. Well, at least the tool was safe. I hoped it would open back up, but I'd try it later.

I didn't know if I could reverse all the steps I had already taken, or what would happen if I tried. I decided to trust someone, and that person was Haru. I would have gone to my dad, but he hated risks almost as much as he hated disobedience. I justified it by thinking there wasn't time for discipline. The truth was, I wanted to skip his disappointment entirely.

Haru sat there, listening to my account of getting and hiding the castle. He watched intently as I carefully unwrapped it from my new baseball shirt. Throughout my story, he had the same look my dad did when I showed him the shelf—absolute shock. It was the first time I saw him react without calmness and confidence. I was excited. I had a secret he didn't already know, but now I wondered what this castle was.

"I thought it was just a puzzle. GD had me solve lots of them growing up. What is it?" I asked, seeing his stunned expression. "I can see this is more than admiration for my grandad's work."

"I'm so proud of you for keeping it safe. It's absolutely spectacular. Your grandad was quite an artist."

I had brought a couple of my drawings of Vadina to show him since he knew about the art. He looked at my sketches with evident appreciation. I was especially proud of the one I added color to.

"You are also quite a talented artist. I'll have to add some extra art classes to your studies."

"I'd love that! Thanks."

"Connor, I understand not trusting the Defenders when they came for your belongings. They reminded you of the cruel authority you had been subjected to. I feel honored that you trust me with this now. I need you to trust me a bit more. I will return this to you when we get to New Haven.

I promise I will, but you're right; it needs to be properly packed. I can't let you take it on the transport with you. I need you to trust the Defenders to transport it safely."

"Oh, I trust the Defenders, but Haru, is it more than just a puzzle? Tomorrow, I'll be ten years old. I'll have a job in two years. I've carried all these secrets and items for months now. I even know about the weapons taken out of our basement." He let out a sigh at that statement. "Will I ever be considered old enough to learn exactly what I've been involved with? I can tell this is important, but it *belongs* to me!" I felt my ire rising.

"Connor, I think at this point there isn't anything I wouldn't trust you with. You are the most mature kid I ever met. I haven't gone over your last test yet, but if you're not a Highmind, I need a new test. Don't worry, there is no separation of people here or in New Haven. There are many undocumented Highminds here, but that is a secret you must keep until you are safely in the town.

"Think back on how much stress has been put on you these past months. We don't do that to children. We protect them until they are much older. You won't hold a full-time job until you finish your schooling, and that's many years from now. We strive to build positive, developmentally appropriate experiences so children can grow up with love, academic proficiency, and confidence. But then there's you."

"What do you mean, 'then there's me'? You said everyone has secrets."

"Yes, many adults, like your grandad, have risked and sacrificed much to make this project happen. And kids have occasionally discovered dangerous knowledge, but not like this! Most kids would have buckled under the pressure, but you seemed to have thrived in this very dangerous adult espionage environment. Your grandad saw this potential in you, and he groomed you with just enough training and information to fulfill his sworn duty to the project. He was wise to keep it from everyone and pass it on, but man, that is a lot for a kid to carry. I find it odd that the two of you kept your parents in the dark."

I interrupted him to say, "My dad hates stuff like this. He wasn't even a little curious about the art. He didn't even look at any of it. He shut that shelf as fast as he could. He made me swear not to scare my mom, so I guess he was protecting her."

"I see. Well, he did what he could to keep you all safe when he found out. There are all kinds of bravery, and he showed the protective kind. But you, you are as cool and clever as a fox. Although you have kept your cool, I suspect it's been very frightening and lonely. You have carried a lot on your shoulders. When I worry about this scary world, I lean on my faith. It reminds me that I'm not alone.

"You aren't alone either, Connor. I will always try to be there for you, but God has been with you through it all, and He always will be. He knows your heart and every one of your secrets, and He loves you no matter what you go through or do. We can talk more later, but we have a Hold to pack up. I'll take care of this."

"Okay," I said, eyeing my castle as I stood up to leave. I didn't fully understand this faith stuff yet. It sounded too good to be true. I'm not sure how to trust an invisible hero, but I trusted Haru. "I'm trusting you to keep your promise to give it back. I want to solve the last steps." I hoped I hadn't turned it over to the authorities, and I was looking at it for the last time.

"Connor, believe me when I say, you will get to solve the last step of this beautiful puzzle."

They need me, I thought. There is something in there, and it's more than congratulations. Holy crap, what have I been carrying around this time?

CHAPTER TWENTY-FOUR

Within five hours, curtains came down leaving cots and luggage exposed and parked around the yard. The rest of the Hold was almost completely dismantled. The night before departure, people were instructed to wear their older clothes so the rest could be packed. We packed the bed frames and put our mattresses on the floor, so they could be quickly loaded tomorrow morning.

The kitchen made sacks of food for the rest of the meals to last until our arrival. Boxing up the toys caused some of the younger kids to complain and whine. It made me realize we had changed enough to be accustomed to a life that goes beyond full bellies and being respected. Four weeks ago, we would have been too afraid to ask for anything extra, let alone expect it. Those assigned careers involving children took care of the young ones, but a lot of us older kids wanted to help pack up. We were accustomed to working, and we wanted to feel useful.

It was early the next morning, and we had been inside for almost four weeks. We were scheduled to leave at sunrise, and we had packed our totes, tablets, and unfinished projects. All the kids were given their own e-book tablets and headphones. Before we left, we were allowed to download two apps for the ride. There was a variety of choices from children's educational activities, challenging puzzles, stories, role-playing games about free communities, and all kinds of videos. I discovered a collection of actual sports events. I downloaded a recording of a real baseball game with professional ballplayers from the past. I also downloaded one of the role-playing games that featured dragons. I was excited and couldn't wait to watch and play them.

We were let outside under the big sky, crunching through the snow, into the emerging sunshine. I drank in the sight of the blinding light and felt the breeze float through my hair. I understood the importance of not going outside the compound, but it felt good to be out in the open on a gorgeous autumn day. I never heard anyone complain about being confined because, ironically, we all knew being locked up was the price of safety and freedom. Slowly, we lined up while soaking in every delectable moment.

They told us when we entered the transport that it would be like the first time. We must be quiet while traveling. The engines were outfitted with sound maskers, but voices were still detectable. The Defenders said that sound detectors could still be encountered on the road. I should be concerned by the warning, but I couldn't wait to watch the game with my new tablet and headphones.

There were lots of people already loading into the three transports from the other three buildings. Each transport held sixty-four seats, with small aisles on both sides to walk down. I got into my seat and began the video of the Kansas City Royals and the Oakland A's in the 2014 wildcard game. I picked it because it had the most innings on the list. This will be the first professional game I have ever seen in a sport I adore. It was going to be epic.

I was so in tune with the game, I couldn't believe the trip was already over. I didn't want to stop. It was an amazing contest. I had to turn it off with the score of Kansas at 3 and the A's at 7.

Before being let out of the transport, the Defenders gave out directions. "Look around and make sure you have all your belongings. When you leave the transport, go directly with the lead Defender to be briefed."

I had hoped to be outside again, but the transports were backed into a loading dock. We were led into a large round room with a glass paneled ceiling. The clouds were gathering and billowing against a royal blue sky. The room was empty of seating and any furnishings, so we stood waiting for instructions.

A well-dressed woman strolled in and wandered among the new citizens. She shook hands, talked briefly with individuals, and occasionally knelt to give the children a rare treat. It was a hard red ball, and it tasted like strawberries. After several minutes, she made her way to the edge of the room.

"Welcome to New Haven!" The speaker stretched out the simple statement to symbolize the lengthy journey and the moment it encompassed. "My name is Carolyn Riddley, and I am the town Recreation Director. You are at the west entrance of our town. I know you are anxious to see your homes and get them settled, but humor me for a moment. I want to describe your new town.

"For weeks, you lived in the Hold with forty to fifty residents plus staff. Our town has a population of well over four hundred people." Gasps could be heard from the crowd. "Around 170 of those are children from ages zero to eighteen. Everyone has responsibilities, including those children.

"We have three schools: one for 0 to K, another for first through sixth, and the last one for seventh through graduation. At night, those classrooms are used for continuing education, group counseling, and other gatherings.

"There are, as you have learned, many occupations and buildings where the employees meet. We have dining areas that are much nicer than you had in the Hold. Mini farms are at the end of each tunnel where we grow small livestock and gardens."

A hand shot up.

"Can I guess your question? You're wondering what tunnel this is." The hand went down, and the questioner nodded her head. "We are in the old

Eisenhower Tunnel. Now, before you get nervous, I want to let you know it is NOT toxic. That story has allowed us to secure this structure and make improvements. It is a continuing secret that will protect us from harm and allow us to grow and flourish without outside interference."

It wasn't very long ago that the story about the massive radioactive waste accident in the tunnel was big news. Even I remembered it. GD talked about that at dinner one night. I guess it was a hoax to keep people away.

"The airflow systems were updated with smaller, more efficient units. The smaller units allowed us to raise the ceiling and build two-story-high structures to conserve space. We have our own power grid and water source. Each side of the tunnel was increased in size by 33 percent. And besides the small area between every other home, we have a nice sized park next to each school. Three corridors connect the tunnels for quick access to the other half of town.

"Our system of government will be explained in the next week or two by your temporary district representatives. The date and time will be announced soon.

"Please follow Noah Ransom," she pointed to a young man standing by a door on the opposite side of the room we came in. We were finally going into the town.

CHAPTER TWENTY-FIVE

While the next group was brought into the skyroom, we were led through a corridor with several tables. My family and I came to the first one where they did a routine med scan. Two people sat behind the next table, and we gathered around to listen to the woman as the man removed our old bands.

"This is a communication and credit band, which we call a CC band. It's removable," the lady explained as she showed us how it snaps. "You should have this on whenever you leave your house. If you aren't wearing it, a beeping sound will ring when you open your door. With this, you can store people's numbers and call them. It also stores your credits, opens your house door, and you can call for help wherever you are."

"Wow! I get credits?" I asked. "Can I call anyone, anywhere? How do I get people's numbers?"

"These only work in the tunnel," she smiled. "A directory to find numbers will be loaded onto your tablet sometime today. You are allowed to spend credits, but they are controlled by your parents, so that will be up to them."

At the other stations, pictures were taken for records and adult work badges, and children were registered for school at the last one.

There was a line for the transportation that would bring us to our new homes. I was super excited to see one of GD's designs. One by one, electric carts drove up towing trailers with two benches that faced outward. The transportation, which was called a bus, could accommodate eight citizens at a time. Other buses with open trailers collected our gear to be dropped off at our addresses. Teke and his family were on our bus, and we filled all eight seats. We came out of the corridor and got our first look at the town.

All the buildings were two stories and tucked against the inside wall. The area in front was used for small patios and traffic. Many people were already riding bikes and walking about. It made me wish I had one of the scooters from the Hold. Half of the people arrived in New Haven a month ago. I knew we would be in shipping container homes, but I hadn't broadened my vision to the grand scale of a whole town. The driver told us it was two parallel tunnels, each fifty feet wide and a mile and a third long.

I imagined dull industrial boxes for homes and a couple of other buildings. The combinations and arrangements of the containers were attractive and diverse. Turning twenty-foot containers perpendicular to the main section produced an L-shaped structure, providing a section for the stairs and utility areas while creating an inset porch at the entrance.

The outside walls still had the ribbed structure of shipping containers, but it added a shadowed texture and it complimented the freshly painted color schemes. Tasteful combinations of neutral tans or greys were painted on one building and interrupted by rich brick and cream tones on another. Some had two containers joined at right angles, forming a nice little cove in between. I noticed the decorative pieces added outside the houses and work buildings.

As we rode, the brightness of the tunnel astonished me. The tops of the side walls were gently rounded and gave an open feeling because the absence of corners made the light reflect evenly. I began to wonder what it looked like at night. I asked the driver.

"It's actually kind of cool. First, the paint has a luminescent shimmer to it, so the lights bounce off it in a diffused glow. We also have four different colors of lights, and they're mixed to create different effects for different times of the day. So, we have sunsets and sunrises. Cool, huh?"

"Yeah, really cool." I wondered who incorporated all these wonderful details with the sole purpose of making us happy. I remembered a signature on the house designs, Alec T., so maybe it was him. I was curious if it would be possible to search for people by name, or if names were still confidential like in the Hold. I wanted to find out to say thank you. And I wanted to find Hayden. Please let him be here.

We came to our house first. Stepping off the bus, I looked up at the two-story house painted in gray-blue and crisp white trim. My mom chose the colors of Grandad's house. The L-shape walled in a small porch with a little balcony above the front door. A big picture window centered on the main room downstairs revealed grey drapes with a hexagon pattern. On the side of the house, was a shared yard with a sliding glass door that mirrored the neighbor's with the same design. This is where the giggling girls lived.

My dad used his CC band, and the door opened. Everything was new and crisp. We walked in on the wood-patterned laminate flooring. They were a white-washed grey, being subtle but mesmerizing at the same time. The walls were off white with dark blue trim on the edge of the floor. A small white table with four matching chairs sat near the front window. I imagined doing my lessons and watching the town go by. Several crates containing our possessions from so long ago sat on the far wall. I didn't see GD's desk. Maybe it held secrets too, and they had it.

A grey couch and two lounge chairs were parked against the back wall. It would make the perfect place to get lost in the tons of books I wanted to read. Three side tables waited to be returned to their mirrored positions on either side of the sofa and between the comfy chairs. But the crates would need to be unpacked and removed first.

As warned, there was no kitchen, but there was a long counter on the back wall with a water cooler. Also on the bottom floor was a large bathroom with a compost toilet, shower, counter with two sinks, and a laundry room with a table and washer/dryer combo. I wondered if I would be doing the laundry again when my parents went back to work. But how hard could pushing buttons be? Where would I take the compost to? I had so many questions.

The three bedrooms were upstairs, connected by a hall. I slid open the drapes matching the front window to find a sliding glass door leading to the balcony. Just a few steps down the hall was a pocket door to the first bedroom. When I entered, I knew immediately it was mine. There was GD's desk against the far wall, and next to it was a shelf. Even though it wasn't built into the wall, I pushed on it. It didn't slide, and it made me laugh. I sat in the new chair and spun it around to take in my room. When I saw the opposite wall, I was shocked to see the U.S. flag from my grandad's shelf and a collage poster of lots of baseball players tacked up on the wall. Was that Haru or Officer Gray, I wondered?

Next to my desk was a twin bed against the stairway wall, with a night-stand and a reading light hanging over the headboard. On the wall adjacent to Meshka's room, sat a dresser with a closet next to it. Inside the closet was a stool to reach the top shelf. They thought of everything. A fluffy, bright red and blue comforter with white piping around the edge lay neatly on my bed. A long window sat high above my desk. It confused me because I knew it was against the edge of the tunnel. I grabbed the stool and pulled open the blinds. A daylight glow came up from the ground floor. Whoa, I thought, that's a nice touch.

I got down and opened the top drawer of the dresser. Inside was a baseball cap with a note that said, "Happy Birthday Connor, and thanks for teaching me about baseball. When we all get settled in town, we should watch a game in the movie room. Your friend, Officer Gray." I forgot it was my birthday. The only time we noticed it was when my age meant some form had to be filled out. The hat had an eagle emblem on the front . I immediately put it on, and it fit perfectly. I was bubbling over with happiness and laughing at the irony of finally getting a hat to block out the sun.

Mesh's room's bedding had a white, green, and lavender design with white ruffles. She also had a desk, shelf, and a window on the back wall. She was playing with her tablet on her bed.

"I love it. It's the best room I ever had. The beds are so flat and comfy. Do you like yours?" she said.

"It's perfect." She got up and came with me to check out our parent's room. Their door was near Mesh's, and a short hall inside it led to a room larger than ours. It was decorated in sage, blue-grey, and off-white. They had two windows that faced the street. My mom was crying happy tears while my dad hugged and kissed her cheeks.

I grabbed Meshka's hand, and we walked out onto the balcony. We sat in the two chairs and watched the people go by. I loved this balcony. I was deep into my thoughts of ways to spend time here and all the other new places just in our house alone.

"Condorman!" I jumped! It was Hayden! He was here!

"HAYS!" I shouted so loudly that people turned and stared. I ran down the stairs as fast as I could, while tears of pure joy welled up in my eyes.

Mesh was following me. "I wanna see Savannah, too!"

"How did you find me so quickly?" I said, hugging him off the ground as soon as he was within reach.

"I was told you would arrive today and what your address was. Haru wrote me a message that I only received yesterday. It said you were coming to live here at this address."

"You got a hat too," I said, noticing it was identical to mine. "Man, I missed you so much. I was afraid I'd never see you again." I was holding back the tears, but when he got choked up, we both started weeping and hugging again.

"Yeah," Hayden said, adjusting his hat and recomposing himself when we broke apart. "Officer Gray said he was thankful I had kept a secret about my dad hiding computer components. I caught him stuffing them in our attic one night."

I was overcome with joy, and so was he. I was excited to tell him all the things that had happened. We had a ton of catching up to do and some baseball to play.

Hayden said he lived on the Southeast side at 107. He had to go back home because Maylee said he should give us time to settle in, but he promised to tell Savannah that Mesh couldn't wait to see her.

I spent time settling into my room, and I helped my mom and dad when I was done. We all sat at the table, going over the things that had just been downloaded onto our tablets. There were instructions for the appliances, our dining hall assignment, and various schedules. We found the contact directory, but you had to know the person's name and last name. I never learned Hayden's last name. It wasn't wise to share unneeded information. The coolest thing was the map. It showed the whole town, and I could zoom in on places to go and learn about them.

I wanted to say hi to Jilly and see how she was doing. I knocked on the door, but there was no answer. I knew we were the last group from the Hold, so the whole town was here now. It seemed weird because they should have been here by now. I would think they would be unpacking and getting moved in. But I thought of the line in the corridor, or maybe they had to go somewhere else. I smiled at the reference. I decided to come back after lunch. Just as I turned to go back home, the pretty bride called to me from her balcony.

"They aren't there." I could tell she had been crying.

"Where are they?"

"You should ask your parents." And she went back inside.

I ran into the house and I saw my mom and dad at the table. Dad had his notebook open, and my mom's eyes were red-rimmed and puffy. "What happened to Jilly?" I demanded.

"We aren't sure," my dad said sadly. "All we know is just before they got on the transport, three Drangers attacked. Witnesses said both Jilly and Ari were hit with bullets, but Officer Gray was in full gear and shooting back. The transport had to leave them there. But Gray was with them, and he's a very decorated Defender. If anyone could save them, it would be him."

One friend returned and two more were taken. She told me she was afraid this would happen. She must have been so scared.

"Look, we just don't know. It could be okay. The word is we will have an absolute answer within a day or two. Don't give up on them."

My heart was breaking again, and I thought about what they had already lived through, what we all have lived through. These women had this happen before, and Jilly almost died, but she's a fighter. I ached that what she was afraid of had come true.

I was miserable. This cycle of being beaten down and fighting to recover had been on repeat for what seemed like years, but it had only been three months. I hadn't finished unpacking yet, but I told my parents I wanted to take a walk. I don't remember where I went, and I didn't notice anyone or any place. I just kept putting one foot in front of the other. Someone stepped in front of me, and it was Haru.

"How is your garden today, Connor? Looks like you need to do some weeding. Are you worried about the residents who were attacked today?"

I nodded . "It's like it will never end."

"Can I walk with you for a few? Talking can help you sort this out."

"I feel like I get up and I get knocked down, then I get up again, and wham. I'm tired of believing because it hurts more when the next hit comes. It was easier when I didn't have hope, when I didn't know how good it could be."

"Hope is a powerful thing. It makes life worth living and worth fighting for. But the biggest thing to remember about hope is that it requires appreciation. You can't have everything go your way. You have to count your blessings, and that gives you hope. And hope gives you the strength to fight through your troubles. For me, faith is the answer. I feel like I'm part of something good, and I'm not alone."

I looked up at him. "I can try. I want to, but it's hard." I knew what he was doing. He's the minister, and he was inviting me to attend church. It used to be forbidden, but it's not now.

"Very hard, but I'm here to help. You just have to ask."

CHAPTER TWENTY-SIX

The next day, I met Hayden at the Recreation Center. I introduced him to Teke, and he introduced me to Kato. Hannah, the Defender who talked to me in the infirmary, was helping Carolyn Riddley. Ms. Riddley worked on getting the center up and running, while Hannah was checking out equipment, and she helped us check out three scooters. Hannah said there were lots of extra jobs available, and we could earn our own scooters if we volunteered. We all decided to volunteer tomorrow, but today we were going to tour this town.

We crossed the midway corridor in front of the hospital. Hayden pointed out the Rapid Aid Station, or RAS, which also held the dentist's office. We continued past a bunch of houses to our new school. Mesh and I had already checked out the playground next to it when we took a walk after dinner. The next building was the Engineering Building. It was where people came up with new things and ways to fix problems.

We reached the west end and rode up to the window. It was a walled-off area where chickens and rabbits roamed in two areas with a wire fence between them. The animals wandered around, pecking and thumping at each other through the fence line. We drove through the west corridor, and Kato pointed out the movie room.

"Officer Gray told me they'll show baseball games," I said.

"Gosh, I hope so," Hayden smiled.

The southwest side of the ranch had goats, and they were playing and leaping in their home. We passed the Waste Management place where the compost toilets and trash get processed. Kato said there is a little door on the side of our house with access to the compost container. People from maintenance came and collected it every few days, so we never had to deal with it. This place just gets better and better.

After that were more houses and a dining hall. The Gym was for people to get exercise, and then we passed the hospital again. The next school was for kids over twelve. It had a huge grassy area for sports games.

"I thought you'd like this," Hayden said. "We can check out baseball equipment and play here."

I nodded with wide-eyed approval. Kato added, "It's softball because the tunnel is too small for hardball. But it's still fun and better than we had before," Hayden explained how they close it off for games needing lots of room. Both ends of the park were fenced to the top of the tunnel. Swinging gates were open for traffic, but during scheduled games, they could be closed off too. Even the lights were guarded by wired grates. My mind started thinking about totally closing this place off and hitting balls here, even if it was a bit small to play a regular game.

"That will be amazing," I said. I thought of how happy it would make GD to know baseball had some new fans.

We drove past more houses, and next to another dining area was the museum. Hayden said it wasn't open yet because it was taking longer than expected to finish everything, and we arrived several days early. I couldn't wait to see Vadina again, and I told the story to my friends. Everyone had participated in building the town in some way, but only Hayden and I were aware of it before we got here. He pointed out the Security Building, and the next place was a tavern. It was a place where adults could hang out together. It wasn't open yet either.

We reached the northwest end of the tunnel. It was a lot like the ranches in the south end, but it was a garden. There were rows of plants with a little stream in a swerving oval pattern through the farm. Fish swam in a man-made current. They went through the corridor to the northeast end of the tunnel and saw a mirror image with different plants and species of fish.

"Wow, these guys thought of everything!" Teke stated.

"It took a lot of people to make this place happen," Kato added.

"I'm very proud I belong to this town, and I'm really glad I don't have to keep secrets anymore," Hayden said.

"I haven't been here long, but it feels like the place my grandad described. I want to belong to this town forever because I'm so proud of it." We all knew it would be discovered someday, but I didn't want to ruin the mood.

The next building was the daycare place. And after that was a large brick building called the New Haven Town Hall. Hayden said the residents would be voting soon to choose the group of people who would lead the town.

"That's where my mom is going to work. It's going to be run the way GD said a fair government is supposed to work." He would have loved this place, this place he sacrificed everything to get to. I knew he'd be happy we made it, which made it even sadder that he didn't. At that moment, my grief became raw and intense like I had lost him all over again, and my melancholy thoughts turned to concern for Jilly and Ari. I put my mood in check. I was with my friends, and every one of us knew loss all too well. This wasn't the moment to spill it out all over the place.

We peeked inside the closed part of the recreation room, seeing all sorts of table games, but it wouldn't be fully open for a week. The other side was open for checking out stuff. It's where we checked out the scooters, so we stopped in, borrowed some softball equipment, and headed to the big park.

On the way, I saw Alicia. She had found some girls her age, and I figured she would be hanging out with them now, so I just waved. School would be opening in a week, and we would meet more kids our age. We threw the ball and talked about everything, including Jilly, Ari, and Officer Gray, because it was allowed now. And we could say it sucked because it did.

"I'll miss the sky, but it's not hard to give up all the horrible stuff that comes with it," said Teke.

"Yeah, but we have that cool skyroom, and we get to watch movies and go to school," Hayden added.

"I bet someday we'll get to go outside again." I believed it could happen because I've seen that good things come our way when we believe in them.

The next evening Billy ran over with the news of Jilly and Ari's rescue. She told us the whole story. "After they were shot, they blacked out. Gray was uninjured due to his protective gear. He took out those Drangers and got Ari and Jilly back inside the Hold using a luggage cart. A doctor and nurse were packing the last of the equipment and found what they needed to treat them in the infirmary. They couldn't be moved until they were in stable condition. The best part is they're going to be okay!" she did a little happy dance. "They have to stay in the hospital for a couple more days, and then they can go home."

I was beyond happy. "Thank you," I said out loud to whoever could hear me.

My mom and dad went to see them the day after they heard they were here. I was told I would have to wait until they came home. The day after the good news, I stood outside looking up at the hospital windows, but I couldn't see inside. It was a long, two-story building painted slate blue and mint green. The colors looked gentle, and I remembered how nice the doctor in the Hold hospital was to me.

"Connor," Gray drove over to me in a security cart, "you know, they are going to be as good as new. There is no need to grow any weeds over it."

"Did Jilly tell you about that?" I wondered how many people knew about it.

"Yeah, it's a cool way to think about worrying."

"Thanks, Officer Gray. I know she'll be okay on the outside, but she told me how scared she was when that guy attacked them while walking to the transport. She said it gave her nightmares, and sometimes she would relive it when she was awake too. Like PTSD, the post-traumatic stress disorder, we learned about in the Hold. This may make it worse, and I just want her heart to be okay."

Officer Gray had a hurt look as he nodded his head. I could see he cared about her a lot, so I decided to change the subject. "I can't wait to go to school, play sports, and do the other stuff around this town. My friends and I rode all over yesterday. It's like a dream. It's nice to be welcome everywhere and not be a Daily anymore. Let me know when you want to play catch or watch a game in the movie room. Maybe a couple of my baseball fan friends could come. Oh yeah, thanks for the baseball cap and for saving them. Especially Jilly, I really like her."

"You're welcome for the hat. How about we throw a couple on Sunday morning, say 10:00? As far as saving Jilly, that was my pleasure."

It was the next morning, and the sisters were coming home. Everyone was gathered in their yard to welcome them. They were surprised when they saw everyone waving.

"This is your house! Isn't it pretty? And we share a yard, just like we hoped." Billie, the bride, said as they looked at their new home for the first time. I looked around for Gray, and then I saw him standing off to the side alone. Jilly saw him and went over to him. He looked sad, and she looked tired. They only talked for a few seconds, and he turned and walked away. She watched him leave and never took her eyes off him until he was out of sight. I watched her go inside, and I went to tell her welcome home, but I didn't stay long. I'll wait to talk to her tomorrow.

It was later that night, and Officer Gray came to my house to talk to me and my parents.

"So, I found your dog, Connor."

"Oh, my gosh! Are you kidding?"

"Well, she lost her collar, and we didn't know she was yours until the other pets had been claimed. Hold on a minute, bud. Here's the change-up." I smiled at his baseball reference. "You need to get permission from your parents and the neighbors on both sides of you. And your parents need to fill out this form." He laid the papers on the table, told us good evening, and started for the door. I followed him out.

"Do you want to go with me to ask Jilly?"

"No way, dude, that's your job."

"She likes you. I can tell. When you left today, she watched you all the way to the corner. She looked sad. You should talk to her."

He laughed, "So you're a matchmaker now, huh? Well, adult relationships are complicated."

"Yeah, my grandad warned me not to get a girlfriend until I'm older and wiser."

"Yep, good advice. I'm still waiting for more wisdom, I guess. Good luck with your parents and your neighbors. As I heard the tale, not even your parents knew about this dog."

"That's true. I lied to them, but I must be pretty lucky because I ended up here. I found my friend and you guys are all okay. Let's hope I haven't used my luck up."

CHAPTER TWENTY-SEVEN

My parents sat down with Mesh and me, and we divided the chores for taking care of Libby. The paper sat on the table unsigned for the whole talk, but they finally signed it. Next, I saw the neighbor girls, Mandy and Mel, in the backyard, and I got permission from them and their mom. They made me promise that they could play with her. I could tell by the way they talked about it they were going to spoil her and turn her into a lapdog.

That just left Jilly and Ari, and I had been waiting for what seemed like an hour for them to come back from breakfast. As soon as they got home, I gave them two minutes to get settled, and I ran over and knocked on their front door. As soon as they opened it, I started telling them the news.

"Slow down, Connor. I can barely understand you," said Ari.

"I get my dog! She's nice and fun, and Mesh and I miss her so bad." I paused briefly to add the more difficult part. "But my mom and dad say if you don't want a dog around, I don't get her. Please don't say no!"

They smiled at each other and invited me in. Jillian offered me a seat at the table and said, "Okay, Connor. Tell us about your dog."

"Her name is Libby, and she's a girl, and the vet lady said she's a terrier. She's small, only this high." I held my hand above the floor to show them how big she was. "She's over a year, but not two. I found her. She was hungry and had a hurt paw. Mesh and I took care of her in secret. When the Defenders came, I asked them to take her. I said please a bunch of times and Mesh cried. They took her, but I didn't know if I would see her again."

"Wow, that's quite a story. Do you have her now?"

"No, I haven't even seen her. But Officer Takota," I used his formal name, so I didn't get involved in their whatever, "he said he'd bring her if my parents and neighbors said okay."

Ari asked me some questions, and I was worried she was going to say no. "So, will you take good care of her? Clean up after her? Where will you get dog food?"

"Don't worry, I'll clean up after her and keep her from barking, and not let her in your yard. And I can get food for her from the kitchen when I go to eat. That's what they told me."

Ari looked at Jillian, and they grinned at each other. "There's only one more question." Ari paused for several seconds while I waited with pleading eyes. "Can we go when you walk her sometimes?"

"Yes! Whenever you want!"

"Well, I guess we are getting a dog for a neighbor."

I jumped up all excited, and they did too. I hugged them before I remembered they were injured with gunshot wounds. It was odd that they didn't even flinch. We must have incredibly good doctors here. "Thank you, thank you!"

I ran out the door with the signed paper, and I heard Jillian yell, "Bring Libby by when you get her." I held my thumb up and ran with absolute joy.

I ran through the mid-corridor and down the street to the security office. I was still out of breath when I asked for Officer Gray at the desk. When he came, I handed him the paper signed by my parents and the two from my neighbors.

"So, your luck held out. Good for you. I had a feeling you would pull it off. Let's get Libby."

"You know, her real name is Liberty," I said.

"I like it. You should call her that. It suits her." I thought we would have to go to one of the farms, but Officer Gray opened the door and whistled. Liberty came bounding out to see me. She remembered me. She had gained some weight, and her eyes were bright and healthy as she bounced around on her paw like it had never been injured.

They gave me a leash and showed me how to walk her on it. I walked her home, and I could tell they had worked with her. When I got home, Mesh was jumping all around. The maintenance crew was already installing a four-foot fence with a gate to enclose our shared yard. Libby was happy to see us, but when my dad scooped her up, I could see she melted right into his heart. I think he missed his dog and had always wanted another one. We decided to take her for a walk together.

School started that next Monday, and I wore my tan cargo pants and red Henley shirt. When we had picked out our clothes, they measured our feet, and new shoes were dropped off at everyone's house the last couple of days. Mine were tennis shoes, and they were super comfortable. I had never had new shoes before, and these fit me perfectly.

Our teacher was named Miss Naddly. There were fifty-one kids in our school and eight in my grade. Alicia and Teke were in my class, but Hayden and Kato were younger and at different levels. Miss Naddly played introduction games and gave us work on our computer desks. We watched a movie about the oceans, read a story about a dogsled team, and studied our town map. We also had an emergency drill that showed us where to go in different situations. We practiced it four times, so we got fast at it. We would have them regularly, she said, but it should make us feel safe knowing there was a good plan.

There were two lunches. The youngest grades went to lunch first, and the older kids went second. At lunch, we walked to the dining hall, and then we played in the yard between the school and the dining hall.

On Thursday, we were told our school would be the first group to visit the museum. Jillian had agreed to go on a walk with me and Libby. It was early in the evening, and we headed east toward the farms. I told her all about fourth grade. I was so excited to be back in school, and I think my words spilled out faster than she could listen.

"And I love lunchtime too because after we eat, we get to play at the park every day! I found my friend Hayden, and my mom says he can come over this weekend, and we can play with Libby! Hey, Jilly, guess what we get to do tomorrow?"

"I don't know. What?"

"We get to see the museum. The kids get to be first!"

"Oh wow, that is a treat! I wonder if it will be open this weekend for us working folks."

"Hey, I'll ask them."

"Thanks, Connor," I told her about the art shelf and my grandad. She said my grandad would have been very proud of me, and she said she was too. It meant a lot to hear her say that.

On Friday morning, we began our walk over to the museum. Mr. Alex Waller met us outside. Rows of chairs were set up in a cove area outside. Mr. Waller, the guy in charge, taught us how to behave in a museum. His helper, Alex, brought the first, second, and third graders in, while Fin spoke to us. He showed pictures on a screen of some of the things we would be seeing. None of them were the dragon, and my heart sank. Fin said they had lots of art, and they would trade it out every month or so. I raised my hand and asked when everyone else could visit the museum. He said it would be open on Wednesday for everyone, but the curator, Mr. Waller, had a few more things to settle in.

When it was our turn, we were led to the history room that displayed America's beginnings and expansion periods.

"And here is a famous ring," Alex pointed at the small display. "It belonged to a beautiful queen from England. She gave it to Mr. Vogel, and he donated this ring to our museum."

The little pink ring didn't hold much interest for me, and I wanted to move on. We went to the section on recent art, and there she was. Vadina. She was encased in glass, so I could walk around and see all her sides. She was beautiful, and a light shone in her yellow-rimmed dark eyes, and also on her treasure, making little light flecks on the wall it faced. A plaque explained her information, but it offered nothing new to me. It was curious that they had sunk the base in velvet material, and it covered the strange symbols on the bottom. I guess she still had some secrets to keep.

I had everything I could ever want: my family, a new home designed by Grandad, my new town, my friends, my dragon, and my dog. Haru told me he would get the castle back to me next week when it was unpacked. I was finally here at the "Somewhere Else". Where I had hope for a good future. There were so many people to thank. GD always said, "Big A, little e. It meant when good things come my way, show big appreciation, but have little expectation that it will be provided without effort from me.

So many people had fought for this world I get to live in, and some even died. The Jenga tower in our tunnel world stands tall and strong today. And I am determined not to let anyone pick it apart and make it fall. I now understand that the true goal of the game is a warning. Greed and selfishness blind people and addict them to power. It is truth and freedom that stand in their way, so they try to own that too. But they aren't things to be possessed because their spark lives in everyone. And when the spark is ignited, the people will find a way to break free.

We, the people of New Haven, have been bathed in the principles of goodness and liberated to find our own truths. We stand with conviction against immorality and ignorance because we know exactly what we're fighting for and what we have to lose.

That night, I looked around my room and at Liberty sleeping in her little bed. I thought about the journey that I resisted every step of the way. I had doubted my parents and my grandad, and I had doubted humanity.

I've learned faith is believing in something good even when bad things happen. It's having hope when everything seems out of control, and nothing is going the way I want it to. It's being thankful and not giving up. I had a lot of people to thank, but first I knelt, folded my hands, and closed my eyes.

"Dear Lord, thank you for keeping us safe and bringing us to this place. I pray someday all people will find their Somewhere Else. Amen."

New Haven

Highmind Series Book 2

Haru Abar, Head of the Mental Health Department at New Haven, sat at the large conference table in the Town Hall building. He was admiring the intricately made castle in the center of the table. It was painted with stunning detail demonstrating its artist's skill. He was waiting for the other members when he heard the noise in the hall. His ethereal connection to the castle's world was severed. The doorknob turned and in walked Bannon Vogel and Gray Dakota. Bannon was the creator and financial backer of the sanctuary town, and Gray was the commander of the Defender army.

"So, what's up, Haru, and why the secret meeting?" Bannon asked as he sat down at the head of the table. Bannon had been enjoying the relief he felt now that everyone and everything was secured in the tunnel, even though it would take months to be fully up and running. Gray had defeated the threat at the Hold, and there had been no sign they were followed or there was any compromising knowledge of the site. The doors were locked down and the false nuclear accident had been accepted as truth. The nuclear generators they used were performing perfectly and even emitting a faint non-threatening amount of radiation making the story all the more credible. Everyone and everything was secure.

"I need to discuss Alec T. Is this a good time?"

Bannon's cheerful expression turned on a dime, and Gray froze. Bannon looked down, noticing the castle. He was formulating many questions about it, but its prominent placement indicated the meeting was about such answers, so he would wait. "Yes, go ahead."

Gray was still standing in the same position since the mention of the name. He didn't even sit down until Bannon had motioned him to do so. Being in charge of keeping New Haven secure, all breaches were his responsibility, and he had just dealt with a serious break in security at the Hold.

"I have been keeping an eye on the boy, Connor." Haru began. "I just wanted to be sure he wasn't exposed to ongoing sensitive information. He was aware of the boxes of art, weapons, medicines, and architectural plans. Many residents hid such supplies when warehouse raids made it impossible to keep large inventories of critical materials together.

Those things are common knowledge to the residents now that they are allowed to discuss their experiences. But I'm worried about one of the planning papers stamped with the Alec T. signature. That stamp didn't leave the tunnel, and very few people had access to papers stamped with it. It was only used at the highest level to confirm the final approval of plans. It was also a security measure to prevent sabotage. I think Connor saw it."

"What was he doing with it?" Gray asked.

"Good question. He was one of the final approval steps. More than likely, it was a clerical error."

"Okay, I can see that, but do we think Connor noticed it? I mean, he's just a kid." Gray was leaning on his elbows with his hands folded in front of him, awaiting the answer.

"I wasn't worried until I saw his IQ scores. We knew he and his wife had participated in the Highmind experiment when we screened him for the program. The experiment to increase intelligence quotients failed on the participants, but a significant percentage of their offspring displayed extraordinary aptitude, continuing onto subsequent generations. His daughter displayed average intellect, but his grandson displayed incredible High-mind traits even as an infant.

"Connor scored exceptionally high in spatial awareness and hyper-thymesia." Haru saw everyone's questioning look. "Hyperthymesia means his recall ability is off the charts. Other assessments suggest he is also very artistic. He has not had much exposure to art beyond the sketchbook and museum exhibit book he confiscated from his grandfather's desk." Haru opened the folder containing Connor's drawing of Vadina. "This was self-taught over a few months and limited study time."

"These are extraordinary," Bannon said as he passed the papers around. "I'll make sure he has access to art supplies."

"In my visits with him, I saw he possessed an exceptionally mature and methodical approach to problem-solving." Haru picked up the castle gently. "This would be a difficult puzzle for most adults, but he has made good progress on it. He accomplished two of the steps at his Fairplay home and one more while in the Hold during the few moments he had to himself because I designed the Hold to maximize social time. It was a challenge to find a place or a time to be alone.

"I bet he needed the flashlight he borrowed from me for one of those steps," Gray speculated as Haru put the castle near him for his inspection.

"No doubt," Haru went on. "His grandfather groomed him to hide his mental abilities. He also taught the exact lessons required to solve complex intelligence clues. I believe," Haru said while pointing, "this castle contains a clue to the whereabouts of Cali Bantu"

Time stopped as the full weight of his statement set in. The stillness of the room was deafening while intense stares bore through the castle before them.

Haru continued. "was a top-notch architect, and he belonged to the underground group involved in Cali Bantu. We don't even know exactly what Cali Bantu is, but many believe it is a powerful weapon. Whatever it is, we need to find it first."

"You could be right," Bannon said, finally breaking the spell that hung in the air. "I remember meeting him, and he said he knew my father. My dad's diary said he never knew the location of Cali Bantu, but he knew some of the people who held pieces of that knowledge. He never disclosed any names, though. No one person knew it all. He used to say, 'The information will come from the pure of heart when the world is ready.' I used to laugh it off, thinking it was one of his political platitudes. Maybe it was a literal forecast or a plan to pass it on to the next generation. So, you believe Connor knows something about Alec T. and perhaps holds the key to the location of Cali Bantu?"

Haru nodded his tilted head with a regretful look on his face. "It's a lot for a young child to bear. He taught him how to conduct a thorough search for answers and evidence, which is why he discovered the shelf. He taught him the story of Camelot, so he could unravel this puzzle. Connor has a keen awareness of his surroundings. When they removed the weapons and medicines from the concealed basement, he watched it happening through a mouse hole. With his sharp mind and enhanced memory, there is little doubt he missed a name on a document he was curious about. And even if he didn't pay attention to it then, he can recall every detail of the document later."

Bannon leaned back in his chair and tipped his head into his folded hands. Taking a big breath, he let it out in a long puff of air. He sat for several moments with a concentrated look on his face. The wheels in his head were visibly churning over the issue and weighing the possibilities. "Why would he not share that with you or ask about it?"

"He's quite good at keeping secrets. He never brought up anything on his own. His whole life has been one secret after another." Haru had more to say, but Gray piped in.

"What exactly did the note say?" Gray was excellent at predicting human behavior, as well as having a sharp mind for detail himself.

"It was quite simple. 'Approved for construction. Alec T.' I figured he wouldn't care or remember, but today he was looking through the T section of the resident address list on his tablet. It may be just an innocent desire to connect with someone who knew his grandfather. There's no way he knows what A.L.E.C.T. means or how dangerous knowing about it is." Haru was observing them. The three of them were the top rung of the government at New Haven. Someday, when the town was settled, there would be elected officials, but due to the deception that brought them here, this trio was needed to sort out the leftover issues. As honorable as these men were, Haru worried they may never believe they're able to hand over the running of the town, which could morph itself into another oppressive we-know-best governing system. The whole point of A.L.E.C.T. was to restore democracy. They couldn't let each other forget that.

"So, the way I see it, we might need this young man to finish solving the castle and perhaps interpreting what it reveals. And we need to come up with a convincing lie about Alec T. or solicit his confidence," Bannon said, summing up the dilemma.

"Well, as far as the castle goes, we do need him," Gray reported. "Rand looked it over and took an X-ray of it. If we try to pull it apart, it has a vial that probably will destroy whatever it is meant to disclose. If it does provide clues to Cali Bantu, we can't risk losing it." Gray rubbed his temples, remembering how early it was and the security issue he stayed up late last night dealing with. "If we're all agreed, we can send for Connor to settle the castle now."

Bannon picked up the phone seated on the table and pushed the buttons for the Wayther household. "Hi Henry, it's Bannon. I hope I didn't wake you. Oh good. Hey, I know it's the weekend, but I have an idea to run by Connor regarding a wooden castle. Yes, it is nice to have weekends with family. No need to thank me. It was our pleasure. But I need to see Connor for a few minutes at the town hall building. Is he there? Great, thanks. I'll send a cart. It shouldn't take long. Thanks again. Oh, don't mention it.

You're very welcome. Bye." Bannon ended that call and rang his weekend secretary to send a cart to address 90. He'll be here in ten. He had just returned from breakfast."

"For the Alec T. issue," Bannon took over, "we can't tell him it's a country-wide organization to restore democracy, which includes finding and securing Cali Bantu. As I see it, we have three choices. We can say 'he' died, didn't show up to the Hold, or 'he' isn't a real person, and that name was made up so no one had to sign their own name." Bannon suggested.

"I kind of like the last one because it's the closest to the truth. If we say he never made it or died, it could be an interesting story to share and imagine scenarios with his friends, or he may try to find people who knew him. We can't give him a mystery to solve or another secret to clutter up his head." Gray knew personally how irresistible a mystery could be to someone with a heightened sense for detail.

"I think we all like the explanation that Alec T. was what everyone involved signed, so no one knew who we were." Bannon looked around the table. Everyone was nodding their heads and looking at each other.

Haru spoke up, "Okay, so I'll tell him Alec T. was a secret name used by those people in charge to keep them safe. I believe we can ask him to keep it to himself. He has proven he has the maturity for discretionary information. I'll also say I had to ask permission to tell him because it's very confidential. That will appeal to his protective nature."

"Sounds good. Did anyone else see these papers? How about his dad?" Bannon asked, making sure the loose ends were neatly trimmed.

"No, his dad said he didn't even look at them. The impression I got when I spoke with him during his Hold interview was he did everything in his power to avoid knowing any of it. I think he's telling the truth. Everything about his demeanor said he was happy to be rid of everything on that shelf. Henry's tests showed above-average intelligence in mechanical abilities, but not in the Highmind range. He protectively never told his wife anything about the shelf, but of course, she knows what everyone else knows now about the plans and the art," Gray reported.

"Connor, on the other hand," Haru continued, "smuggled souvenirs despite realizing how dangerous it was to know of it, let alone be in possession of it. He's lucky he wasn't caught during the move."

"Hmm, he may be advanced in some ways, but he's still a kid, and he's dangerously territorial about what he deems as his." Gray appeared to be pondering that last thought, "I'll need to keep in touch with this kid. Today, he needs protection, but someday we'll need his skills. Maybe he'll even be involved in A.L.E.C.T. someday."

Just then, a knock came at the door. Haru got up and let Connor in. He was followed by Rand Lewis. They were both offered a seat at the table. Connor was visibly intimidated by the powerful men sitting before him.

Acknowledgements

I remember the day I held my first published book, *Sins of Survival*. I was over the moon with joy. How lucky was I to find a job I love so much? I have since learned the life of an author involves more than creating. There is a business side too. My little book and I joined the thousands of new and yet-to-be-discovered authors in the shark-infested waters of publishers and marketers circling and hoping to bite off a chunk. How ironic that the title of my first book became my new reality. But, I thank them too. It is a necessary part of this endeavor, and I must learn to navigate it.

The learning curve is steep, and it's easy to wear out family and friends. And though the depth of my appreciation cannot be fulfilled in an acknowledgment page, I will attempt it just the same.

I thank my husband, Bryan, for taking on more than his share to give me the time and space to write, and for encouraging me. I couldn't be more grateful for all the time he spent reading and rereading everything, and especially for being my business manager. But I thank him mostly for believing in me and the potential of my work. He's my biggest fan, and he pushes me to continue to write and publish.

Thank you, Bella, my middle school granddaughter, for suggesting I write a book appropriate for young readers. I thank Russ, Ashleigh, Lorraine, Carol, MurlAnn, Whitney, Piper, Becky, Erin, and so many others for engaging in hours of reading, reviewing, and hours of meaningful dialog. I thank my brother, Richard, for encouraging me and giving me free marketing advice.

I want to give a shout-out to Ashleigh for painting this incredible cover, and to Robert Griese of RG Graph X Design for taking my design ideas and formatting the final product. Thank you to all the local businesses that have allowed me to advertise my book. Kelsey's Bar and Grill, Amazon, Barnes and Noble, The Well-Read Moose, Pritchard Tavern, and the CIN library system.

Thank you to all my readers. You make this worth it, which is good because so far I've done more investing than profiting. **I want to thank everyone who wrote a review, and if you haven't please do.** It is the most valuable currency to me as an author. It's not only insightful; many opportunities become available when my books reach 150 reviews.

But mostly, I thank God for giving me guidance, forgiveness, love, compassion, joy, and grace. Through all the times I screamed at my computer, stressed over business issues (why can't I just write, right?), and cried over the terrible hardships I put my beloved characters through, I have never felt alone. I have been blessed with a wonderful life full of good people.

Amen

About the Author

Like most authors, reading and writing are Roxanne's passions. She was heavily influenced by her father's love of literature and science and by her mother's creative spirit. She has an MS in education and was a middle school teacher for twenty years teaching language arts and science. She wrote her first novel, *Sins of Survival,* and published it in 2022. It has adult material, and as a retired middle school teacher, she decided to write a series for young teens. It shares the same setting and characters, so parents and children can read books appropriate for them and share the unique details found in each. Northern Idaho has been her home for over thirty years where she and her husband live on five acres with their border terrier named Nikki.

Visit my website: https//:Roxannewardauthor.com Please leave a review. I read and value every response.

9 798898 001003